WEB OF DECEIT

A good looking man turned up on Louise's doorstep one day, introducing himself as Daniel Kinsella, an Australian friend of her brother-in-law, Greg. He said he had come to stay whilst he did some research — apparently, Greg had written to her about it. Louise's initial reaction was to turn him away, but he was very persuasive. However, she was to discover that Daniel had bluffed his way into her life, and soon she found herself caught up in his dangerous mission.

Books by Margaret McDonagh
in the Linford Romance Library:

MARGARET McDONAGH

◆

WEB
OF
DECEIT

Complete and Unabridged

LINFORD
Leicester

First published in Great Britain

First Linford Edition
published 1999

British Library CIP Data

McDonagh, Margaret
    Web of deceit.—Large print ed.—
Linford romance library
    1. Love stories
    2. Large type books
    I. Title
    823.9'14 [F]

ISBN 0–7089–5471–5

Published by
F. A. Thorpe (Publishing) Ltd.
Anstey, Leicestershire

Set by Words & Graphics Ltd.
Anstey, Leicestershire
Printed and bound in Great Britain by
T. J. International Ltd., Padstow, Cornwall

This book is printed on acid-free paper

For Pauline, with thanks
I stuck at it!

1

Tension and anticipation hung in the air. It was important that they got this right and no-one in the room was feeling particularly relaxed as a result.

'This is our final meeting. You each have an updated copy of the file and have discussed all the relevant information. We've been over the plan. Are we agreed?'

The select group in the small, bare room glanced at each other then nodded their assent to the heavy-set man who sat behind the room's only table.

Norman Curry's cold blue stare appraised them. As he smoothed a hard, veiny hand over his bald scalp, he could sense the adrenalin beginning to flow as they prepared for the challenge they were about to face. He knew that their instincts were razor-sharp. They would need to be.

'I'm not entirely happy with this,' he barked, a frown deepening the lines that furrowed his brow. 'We know practically nothing about what to expect, and that makes me nervous.'

A young man in the back row cleared his throat.

'It won't be easy, Chief. With an isolated cul-de-sac on a private estate surrounded by woods, we — '

'I'm well aware of the problems,' the older man interrupted with evident impatience, the rancour in his voice quelling further comment.

'It is precisely because of the unusual nature of the situation that I'm prepared to run with this plan.' He surveyed those in the room once more. 'Now, is there anything else?'

'We are relying heavily on the initial approach. This project could still blow up in our faces before it even gets off the ground.'

Norman Curry gazed at the man who spoke from the front row, certain the expression in the hazel-green eyes mirrored that in his own — a mix of dislike and grudging respect.

The man was a maverick, a wild card, and Norman was relying on him to pull off this crazy scheme.

He fixed him with a cold, narrowed stare, one which would have intimidated anyone else but failed to bring even a flicker of response to those cat-like eyes.

'Then you'll have to be at your most persuasive,' he growled in answer to the challenge.

'Just acknowledging the risks, Chief,' the man pointed out as he relaxed back in the uncomfortable chair as poker-faced and expressionless as ever.

Irritated, Norman Curry rose to his feet, bringing the meeting to an end. He gathered his papers and maps together and wedged them back in his file before he strode to the door.

'You all know what you have to do. It is time to put Operation Masquerade into action.'

★ ★ ★

Louise Shepherd stretched blissfully, enjoying her first lie in for months. Summer term was over, and she experienced as much pleasure at the release as her students had displayed the previous afternoon. The sense of freedom was wonderful.

Six weeks! She could feel the huge grin spreading across her face. With a deep sigh, she lay back against the pillows.

Apart from a couple of staff meetings and the usual preparation for her classes in readiness for the start of the next school year, she had no-one to please but herself.

As much as she loved the school, her work teaching English and Drama and her inquisitive and boisterous students, the summer escape was special. It was a time to recharge her batteries.

She hadn't planned anything in particular for the weeks ahead, but that was the beauty of it.

For once in her ordered life, nothing was governed by schedules or rigid timetables, the pressure of work or the demands of others. Previous summers had been full and busy — enjoyable in their own way, but she had still been tied to responsibilities, and generally the house had been full.

This summer was for her. With her parents on an extended visit to Australia visiting her older sister, Virginia, her husband, Greg, and their three children, and with no family friends or colleagues of Greg's staying for the summer, Louise had the house to herself. And she was going to enjoy every moment of it!

She could be alone when she wanted to be, could do what she wanted to do when she wanted to do it, could even do nothing at all if she felt so inclined. And if the intense, energy-sapping heat of the last few days persisted, that was a distinct possibility.

Louise slipped from the bed and went

to the bathroom to enjoy a refreshing shower.

The cool spray was a balm to her heated skin, and with delicious relish, she tipped her face to the water. It was heaven. She shampooed her shoulder-length red hair, then snapped off the shower.

After patting herself dry and combing out her hair, she borrowed one of her father's large, cotton shirts that covered her slender figure almost to the knees, then went downstairs to the kitchen and put some coffee on to percolate.

The sun was already high and the house felt stifling. Louise went through opening windows and the patio doors that led to the secluded garden of the family house on the private estate, but there was barely a breath of wind to bring relief.

She could not remember a heatwave this merciless, not in Surrey anyway. Even the windchime suspended from the terrace that usually tinkled melodiously now hung silent and still.

Louise returned indoors, and as she waited for the coffee, she thought longingly of the powerful oscillating fan she knew they had somewhere. All she had to do was find it!

Remembering that the understairs light was faulty, she fetched a torch from the utility room and went back through the house to the hallway.

She shone the beam over the collection of assorted boxes hidden in the depths of the storage cupboard.

'Where is the wretched thing?' she muttered to herself as she edged farther into the tight confines between a stack of boxes and a redundant chest of drawers.

The shrill sound of the doorbell startled her and as she straightened involuntarily, she banged her head on the underside of a stair riser.

'Ouch!' she complained and rubbed her sore head gingerly.

It was bound to be the postman, she decided, and fearing he would be in one of his talkative moods she called out, 'Leave it on the step,' in case he had a parcel.

There followed no distinctive rattle of the letterbox or thud of envelopes on the mat.

Instead, in defiance of her instructions, the bell rang again, more insistently this time. Muttering darkly under her breath, and feeling in no mood for a social gossip, Louise abandoned her search for the fan and backed out of the cupboard.

To her surprise, she discovered there were already a couple of letters on the mat — so why had he rung the bell? He was still there — she could see his shadow through the tiny pane of frosted glass in the centre of the solid front door.

Sighing with resignation, she pulled open the door and instinctively bent to pick up the envelopes.

Her gaze encountered a pair of tan cowboy boots planted firmly on the doorstep.

As she straightened, her gaze

continued slowly up a pair of jean-clad legs, over lean hips and a broad chest to a tanned throat and stubbled jaw. Her gaze passed over a ruggedly handsome face, to clash with a pair of hazel-brown eyes that regarded her with a moment of apparent surprise before their expression became unreadable.

She was vaguely aware that a pair of dark glasses were hooked over the breast pocket of his ocean-blue shirt, and that the Australian bush hat — minus the swinging corks — that was tilted at a rakish angle over his forehead covered thick, dark hair.

Louise's brown eyes widened with bewilderment at the sight of the stranger, and she took an involuntary step backwards.

'I'm sorry. I thought you were the postman.'

'Lucky postman.' Amusement crossed his lips. 'If you always answer the door dressed only in a man's shirt, you must brighten his round every morning.'

A tinge of colour stained her cheeks

at the husky, Australian drawl. Her normal composure rattled, she eyed the man warily.

'What is it you want?'

'Well . . . '

One dark eyebrow rose, and a grin of pure provocation curved his mouth as his feline gaze travelled lazily from her head to her toes and back again.

With considerable effort, Louise resisted the urge to tug the ends of her father's shirt farther to her knees.

'Look, Mr . . . ?'

'Kinsella,' he inserted calmly at her querying pause. 'Daniel Kinsella.'

Louise nodded her head in brief acknowledgement of the information.

'What are you doing here, Mr Kinsella?'

'I've come to stay, Miss Shepherd.'

'What?'

Another amused smile flickered across his face at her horrified expression.

'You weren't expecting me? Greg didn't tell you?'

'Greg? No, I — '

Louise snapped off the words and frowned. Her brother-in-law had not mentioned this to her, blast him, and he knew that she wanted to have this summer to herself, unencumbered by house guests. How could he do this to her? She hung on to her patience and managed a polite smile.

'I'm sorry, Mr Kinsella, there has been a mistake. I'm not able to take visitors this year.'

'I'm staying, that's all there is to it,' he stated matter-of-factly.

'Excuse me?' She stared at him in disbelief. 'Look — '

'It's all been arranged.'

'Not with me.'

'That's not my problem,' he countered in uncompromising fashion as his watchful eyes narrowed.

Louise's jaw set in a stubborn line.

'Mr Kinsella — '

'I am hot, tired and hungry,' he interrupted once more.

With a flick of his hand, he gestured at a hire car now parked in the drive.

'I've had a long flight and then a drive down from the airport. Do we have to discuss this on the doorstep?'

Her gaze dropped to the battered suitcases by his boot-clad feet. She hesitated and chewed her bottom lip. If Greg had sent him . . . With a sigh of resignation, she stepped to one side.

'I suppose you had better come in. Just while we sort this out,' she qualified as he walked through and dumped his bags on the plush, blue carpet in the hall.

He appeared bigger now he was inside the house. An inch or two over six feet, his lithe, hard body filled the passage and his nearness caused a shiver to travel through her body alarmingly.

He swept the bush hat from his head and raised a hand to brush the thick strands of dark hair back from his forehead — all except one wayward lock that curved endearingly across his brow.

His face was strong, determined,

12

with a square, no-nonsense jaw that was darkened with a day's growth of beard.

His mouth was full and sensuous, and his eyes, so hazel, were darkly lashed.

There was nothing soft or gentle about this man. He was direct, intense, uncompromising.

Aware that she was staring, and that he knew it, Louise cleared her throat, edged past him, and led the way to the kitchen. As he sat on a gingham-cushioned chair at the table, she poured him a cup of coffee and set it before him.

'Thanks.' He smiled. 'I need this.'

'Milk and sugar?'

'Black is fine.'

Louise wanted to debate the issue of his presence at the house straight away, not that there was much to debate, she allowed. He was leaving and that was final.

But those hunter's eyes watched her and their unwavering appraisal made her uncomfortable.

Properly dressed, she anticipated she would regain her composure and be able to take control of the situation.

'Please excuse me for a moment.'

She left him to drink his coffee and returned upstairs.

In her room, she pulled her drying hair back in a restraining knot, then discarded the shirt and selected a rose-pink sundress from her wardrobe. As she struggled with the tie fastening, her thoughts turned to the problem of the man in the kitchen, and she cursed Greg for landing her in this predicament.

Her brother-in-law had done something similar once before when he had neglected to inform her that a business colleague wanted to stay for a couple of weeks with his wife.

Their arrival had caught her on the hop. That had been bad enough but Greg knew perfectly well she had plans of her own this summer.

There was no way she could allow

Daniel Kinsella to stay in the house and that was all there was to it, Greg or no Greg.

In determined frame of mind, and prepared to do battle to win back the peace and solitude she had been longing for, Louise squared her shoulders and left her room.

2

Dan twisted the half-empty cup of coffee in his hands, a frown of consideration on his face.

Louise Shepherd had been a surprise. The photograph he had seen of her hadn't done her justice. In it, she had appeared the archetypal teacher, her hairstyle severe, her clothes bland and proper.

She had looked older than her twenty-six years, none of which had prepared Dan for the Louise Shepherd who had opened the front door mere minutes ago.

She was a stunner, no doubt about it — and that shirt had left little of her slender body to the imagination. She was a classic English rose, all clear skin and elegant refinement with a delicate bone structure and luminous, dark brown eyes.

Freed from the confines she had trapped it in, her hair was thick, the colour a rich red that gleamed in the light.

The hint of a dusting of freckles across her nose intrigued him, as did the tempting Cupid's bow of her mouth.

Dan reined in his thoughts and ignored any flicker of personal interest. He had never imagined being attracted to the woman. And he was attracted. It was an unwelcome complication and one he would have to ignore. He had no time for pleasurable diversions.

There was a job to do.

His gaze made a casual sweep of the large, expensively-appointed kitchen, the sunshine-yellow decorations giving it a light and airy feel that was at the same time understated. Everything he knew about the Shepherds and had seen of the house so far, spoke of old money and social standing. A derisive grimace darkened his face.

He heard light footsteps on the stairs, and schooled his expression, hunching his shoulders in tiredness as he returned his attention to the cup in his hands.

Louise halted at the kitchen doorway and watched her unwelcome guest for a moment before he became aware of her presence.

In his early to mid-thirties, he looked casual but respectable but she was still wary of his presence and determined that the mix-up with Greg would not spoil her holidays.

He did look tired, she allowed, and she knew from experience how long the flight from Australia was. No doubt he was also disappointed to discover that the home away from home he had expected to find had proved to be unwelcoming.

Unwilling to allow her sympathy to weaken her resolve, Louise mentally shook herself and walked into the room.

He glanced up as she approached and regarded her changed appearance through weary eyes.

'Would you like something to eat, Mr Kinsella?'

'Dan, please. Some toast would be good.' He gave a wry smile. 'I didn't eat much on the plane. I'm not the best of travellers.'

Louise put a couple of slices of bread in the toaster, then put a dish of butter and a pot of marmalade on the table. She refilled his cup with hot coffee then poured one for herself before the toast popped up. She put the golden slices in a rack before him.

Then she sat at the table and sipped her drink in silence as he ate the first piece of toast.

'I hope Greg not telling you I was coming hasn't ruined your holiday,' he commented after a moment, a sympathetic smile on his face. 'Has that fancy private school you teach at broken up yet?'

Louise nodded and digested the information that he knew what she did for a living.

'Yesterday.'

'Do you have any special plans for the next few weeks?'

'Nothing definite, just a host of things I want to do here.'

He sent her a considering look, the hazel eyes intent, before he glanced away and concentrated on spreading marmalade on his second slice of toast.

'I won't be any bother. I'm quiet and house-trained!'

He flashed a smile. 'I've been looking forward to the peace here to get some work done. I hate hotels.'

His voice was deep and faintly husky, the accent clear and attractive. Louise took another sip of her coffee.

'What line of work are you in? Accountancy, like Greg?'

'No. Imports and exports. I have research to do here and reports to write.'

The information was briskly delivered and his manner made her hesitate to question him further. Clearly he was a man who kept his own counsel. She could sympathise with that.

The problem was that she didn't want him conducting his research or writing his reports in her house.

Only it wasn't her house, she acknowledged with an inward grimace. Her return to live in the family home had been a joint decision, one that had been a godsend to her when she had needed the refuge three years ago, and it now suited her and her parents perfectly.

But the house did belong to her parents, and they did have an arrangement with Greg.

She may be responsible for the property when her parents spent months of each year in Sydney, and although it was her home, too, the decisions rested with them.

Having house guests, friends of theirs from Australia and colleagues of Greg's over on business trips and holidays, was something they enjoyed.

'I'm sorry this has been a surprise to you,' Dan began, cutting across her thoughts. 'But the apparent communication problem isn't my fault.'

Louise hated to admit it, but he was right. It bothered her that she knew nothing about Dan, but he spoke of Greg with an easy familiarity, and she was positive her brother-in-law would never make any kind of arrangement for anyone to stay if they were not trustworthy.

'How long had you intended to stay?' she asked guardedly.

'A few weeks.'

'A few weeks?' she quoted back in alarm. 'But . . .'

Dan pushed his empty plate aside and took a wad of crisp, new, sterling notes from his wallet. He counted some out on the table.

'That should take care of the first fortnight.'

Louise stared at the money, reluctant to pick it up and so signify her agreement for him to stay. Doubts still remained, and she had a lingering unease she was unable to explain.

'How do I know you are who you say you are?'

Dan took his passport from his pocket and slid it across the table towards her.

'I'd suggest you call Greg and check with him, only he's on holiday.'

'Oh?'

'Didn't you know? He and Ginny and the kids have taken your parents up to the Barrier Reef.'

She had known, and that he knew so much about her family, their movements, their names — things he could only have learned through acquaintanceship, allayed some of her suspicions. She glanced at the photograph and name on the passport and handed it back.

'I suppose I could call Greg at the hotel.'

An amused smile curved Dan's mouth.

'You could . . . but I thought they were staying on a boat.'

Louise allowed a small smile in

return as his response gave credence to his claims. He appeared genuine and straightforward, and his persuasiveness had chipped away at her defences. Already she could envisage all her hopes for the summer turning to dust.

Her inate sense of responsibility overrode her own wants. She felt duty-bound to honour the agreement he had made with Greg and, by association, with her parents.

'There are some ground rules,' she explained, resignation in her voice. 'My room and study, and my parents' bedroom and sitting-room, are out of bounds. Otherwise, guests live as family. You see to your own meals unless you wish to make a different arrangement, and you can either buy in your own supplies or pay for what you use here.'

'That sounds fair.'

Louise rose from the table and attempted to disguise how disconsolate she felt.

'Can I get you anything else?'

'No thanks. What I need right now is a shower and a shave, and a few hours sleep.'

'Then I'll show you to your room.'

Dan collected his belongings from the hall and followed her up the stairs.

'It's a big house to be rattling around in on your own.'

She threw him a glance over her shoulder but neglected to mention how much she had been craving just that solitude. Once upstairs, she walked along the landing in the opposite direction from her room. At least he would be out of sight if not out of mind.

Louise opened the door of a spacious bedroom and was about to unfasten the window from which there was an attractive view of the secluded garden and thick belt of trees when she realised Dan had paused in the doorway.

'Is something wrong?' she asked.

'I'm sorry to be awkward, but do I have to have this room?'

'What's wrong with it?'

'Nothing, it's not that. I'd just prefer something with less sun. Have you one that faces north?'

There was one, next to her own, but she was reluctant to have him that close.

Her gaze locked with his, and after a silent battle of wills, she found herself giving way again.

'This way.'

Louise smothered a sigh of irritation and retraced her steps along the landing, past the top of the stairs and along to the far end. There were two doors. The one on the right led to her own room. She opened the door on the left.

'This is perfect,' Dan pronounced from behind her as she stepped inside.

Louise eyed him dubiously. Although it was larger and just as attractively decorated, she thought it the least appealing room in the house.

Although it was cooler, even in summer it could be dark, and the view over the curve of the drive and the house next door to the woods beyond was dull compared with that from the first room she had shown him.

As she opened her mouth to suggest he look at something else, he cast a cursory glance at the window then dropped his bags to the floor, apparently satisfied. Clearly he was not to be moved.

'I'll fetch some bed linen, then.'

When she arrived back from the airing cupboard, Dan had closed the curtains, the room now illuminated by two bedside lamps that sat on twin polished mahogany tables.

One of his cases was open, clothes and a washbag spilling haphazardly from inside. He smiled when he saw her and relieved her of the pile of sheets and duvet.

'I can do this, Louise.'

'Then I'll leave you to settle in. The bathroom is two doors along on the right,' she informed him as she backed towards the door. 'I'll pop down to the supermarket later on and stock up on a few things. You can let me know tomorrow what you want to arrange about meals and supplies.'

'Fine.'

'I'll also put a set of house keys on the table in the hall.'

'Thank you.'

The door clicked shut behind her as she made her way back downstairs. For a while she busied herself with household chores. Upstairs, she heard sounds from the bathroom; footsteps, the shower running, muted whistling, then all was quiet.

Appreciating his need to sleep, Louise left the vacuuming, never her favourite occupation, and went to her study to make some notes of ideas she had for next term.

But she found she could not settle, and it wasn't the heat that was causing her restlessness but the presence of the man upstairs — the disturbing stranger who had turned all her plans upside down in the short time since he had arrived on the doorstep.

Unable to concentrate, she resumed her search for the oscillating fan, but when that proved fruitless, Louise decided she may as well give up all pretence of work.

She would drive to town for a few basic necessities — necessities because there were now two in the house instead of one.

Dan watched from a crack in the curtains as Louise drove her car down the cul-de-sac and turned on to the central avenue of the up-market private estate in the direction of the main road.

It had been easier than he had anticipated.

Louise had taken everything at face value and there had been no need for him to stray from Plan A. Now she had even gone off to do her shopping and left him alone in the house. It had all worked to his advantage, but he discovered to his surprise that her lack of caution angered him.

All right, he allowed, so he was a

cynic by nature, but she was a fool to trust so easily. He moved away from the window. Who was he to complain? That she had played into his hands made his job a whole lot easier.

His skin still damp from his shower, he pulled on a clean pair of jeans and a faded blue T-shirt, then sat on the bed.

The well-worn briefcase he had brought with him rested by his side. He reached for it and released the combination locks, then took a mobile phone from inside.

Dan leaned back against the pillows, a smile of satisfaction on his face as he punched in a number.

The line connected, rang once, and was answered.

'It's me,' he said to the silent listener. 'I'm in. It was a piece of cake.'

3

It was mid-afternoon by the time Louise returned home. She had not intended to be out so long, but she had met a couple of old friends she had not seen for months, and they had shared an impromptu lunch, spending an enjoyable hour catching up on their news.

Afterwards, she had made her usual mistake and loitered outside Guildford's famous second-hand bookshop.

The invisible magnet had drawn her inside, and she had lost track of time. When she had finally emerged, she had a parcel of books she had promised herself she would not buy. It was always the same.

A short journey from the town and through a brief burst of Surrey countryside found her home in the secure tranquillity of The Plantation private estate. She turned into the central avenue, drove past The Oaks and The Ashes, until she reached The Beeches.

A handful of secluded houses slipped by and then she turned into the drive at the right-hand end of the cul-de-sac. The house sign, Woodpeckers, was now weathered and partially obscured by the lush growth of a laurel hedge that screened the house from its neighbours.

From the drive, she glanced upwards and saw that the curtains in Dan's room were closed. The house was quiet when she went inside, so it appeared her unwanted guest was still sleeping off the effects of his flight.

Much longer and it would take him a while to adjust to the different time zone.

But, she allowed, if he travelled often for his work, presumably he knew what suited him best.

Louise put away the groceries, then went through to her study with her parcel of books.

She eyed the overflowing shelves with a guilty grin. She had two major weaknesses, she admitted — books and Cary Grant films.

With a smile, she switched on her CD player allowing the gentle strains of her favourite classical music to drift softly around the room. She set the books on her desk and sat down.

Her smile faded to be replaced by a wary frown of puzzlement. A flicker of unease assailed her.

Quickly, she looked over the notes and papers on her desk, opened the drawers, checked her file tray — nothing appeared to have been touched. Her frown deepened.

She couldn't explain the sudden feeling she had that someone had been through her things. Someone. There was only one someone. Dan.

She rose to her feet and went quietly through the other downstairs rooms. All appeared normal.

The doors and windows were in the positions she remembered them. All her mother's expensive pieces of porcelain were in their proper places, the house keys she had left on the hall table had not been moved, in fact, everything was as she had left it. So why did she have this weird feeling?

Louise glanced down. She could see no tell-tale footmarks in the deep pile carpet — only those she had just made. She had no grounds for her suspicions, but her initial unease remained.

She went upstairs and tiptoed along to her room. Everything was in order as before, she could not find a thing out of place, yet the vague feeling that all was not as it seemed refused to be banished.

Back on the landing, she paused outside Dan's door. No sound came from within, no fragment of light showed under the door, so she silently opened it a crack.

In the dimness, she could see Dan sprawled face down on the bed. The sheet covering him had slipped to his hips, revealing broad shoulders and a tanned expanse of back.

Louise ignored an unwanted flicker of feminine interest. Dan was breathing evenly and clearly asleep.

Softly, Louise closed the door. She went back downstairs to the kitchen and made herself a cup of tea.

What an imagination! She shook her head, a wry smile on her face at her foolishness.

Dan heard Louise's footsteps descending the stairs. What had she been checking just then?

He rolled over and linked his hands behind his head as he stared up at the ceiling. He would wait another half an hour, then put in an appearance.

There were times in his job when his emotions swung from frustration to anxiety, times of boredom — like now, he acknowledged with a grimace — times when sharp wits were called for and he had to think on his feet, adapt in a moment. He hated what he had to do to Louise, hated more that he had feelings about it at all.

It had never happened to him before. He was good at what he did because the people never touched him on a personal level. It was a ruthless streak that helped him do what had to be done. But with Louise, he feared it could become personal.

His briefing had been thorough, and he knew what he had to do. Indeed, he had already begun.

He had made a systematic examination of the house; her desk, the bureau in the sitting-room, filing cabinets, anything he thought warranted attention. His gut instinct had told him what he would or would not find, and his gut instincts were seldom wrong.

Dan scowled and rose from the bed. But he had not gone through Louise's personal things.

He had looked in her room, been unsurprised by the pastel femininity of it, but had withdrawn without inspecting. He was getting soft in his old age and if he wasn't careful, that softness could lead to carelessness.

Carelessness he could not afford.

He drew back the curtains and looked out at the view — a view that adequately suited his purposes.

His introspection continued. It had never bothered him before to invade someone's life, their privacy.

He was clinical. He did what was necessary to get the job done — then he walked away.

It would be wise to remember that.

But for the moment, he had to cement his position here. Then it was a question of watching and waiting.

At least the environment was more comfortable than he was used to, just so long as he didn't get too comfortable.

Dan pulled his T-shirt back on and gave his appearance a brief check in the mirror. A cynical smile touched his lips as he rumpled his hair. He hoped he looked suitably rested.

As he left the room, allowing the door to close with a casual bang, he hesitated on the landing.

The faintest trace of Louise's perfume

lingered, teasing him with the fresh, flowery hint of lilacs.

He went downstairs and helped himself to a glass of water at the kitchen sink, then sauntered through the house.

He found Louise sitting in a swing seat on the patio, engrossed in the book in her hands. He felt an unaccustomed and unwelcome warming of his blood at the sight of her.

'Hi,' he said as he stepped outside, blanking his expression as she looked at him. 'What are you reading?'

She tilted the book towards him so he could see the cover.

'Is it good?'

'Mmm. I've read it before and I love its magic and atmosphere.' She smiled in apparent embarrassment and set the book on her lap. 'You look more rested.'

Dan sat on a chair opposite her and nodded, a teasing note slipping into his voice.

'It's amazing what a couple of hours

in bed in the middle of the day can do for you. You should try it sometime.'

He hadn't expected to make her blush. That she did so easily amused him. He enjoyed it.

Not so the charge of desire that shot through him as he watched the delicate colour wash her cheeks, the way she hid her eyes, the nervous sweep of tongue over lips.

His stomach tightened to knots.

With practised discipline, he suppressed the feelings. Nothing could be allowed to divert him from the job he had to do.

When she looked back at him, he held her gaze and saw a subtle, underlying change of emotions.

The brown eyes regarded him with a guardedness and a glimmer of suspicion that he had not detected before. What had put it there? He had been careful, he always was.

There was no way she could possibly know what he had really been doing while she was out, and yet — guilt was not an emotion that had ever troubled him in the past.

Now, he felt as near to it as he had ever come, although he would not allow any sign of it in his expression.

Louise searched Dan's gaze — she wasn't sure what for. His hazel-green eyes were clear and untroubled, with no hint of guile or guilt, only a sharp intelligence that had previously been masked by fatigue.

Dressed casually in jeans and a fresh T-shirt, he looked attractive. The tiredness had been stripped from his face.

His jaw was clean-shaven and now looked even more determined. His hair was muzzed from sleep, and as she watched, he ran his fingers through the thick, untamed strands in a half-hearted attempt to restore order.

'Have you been out yet?'

The sound of his husky, accented voice startled her from her inspection.

'Yes. Was there something you wanted?'

'I was just wondering about food,' he admitted as he leaned forward and rested his forearms on his knees. 'I understand you are a vegetarian . . . I eat meat. We may have something of a problem here.'

'What you choose to eat is up to you.'

'So you won't mind if I have a juicy steak?'

Louise's eyes narrowed at his mischievous smile.

'Just as long as you don't expect me to cook it for you.'

'No worries!'

'I'm the only vegetarian in the family, so you'll find plenty in the freezer.'

Dan rose lazily to his feet and stretched, making her all too conscious of the lean length of his body.

His teasing smile widened to a grin.

'Thanks. I'm famished.'

Louise watched him walk away and into the house, his stride loose-limbed and deceptive as he moved with cat-like grace. She expelled a shaky breath, disconcerted by her awareness of him. At least he had been open and friendly. There had been no hint that he had anything to hide, no reason for her lingering doubts about him.

All she had to do was put him out of her mind and forget he was here. She swallowed a gurgle of laughter. That was all? Some hope. With an effort, she made herself concentrate on her book.

When Dan emerged from the house a while later, Louise had long since closed her book and given up all pretence of reading.

How could she when her mind was filled with a confusing mix of thoughts about Dan? She glanced suspiciously at the plate of food he was carrying, and he laughed.

'I made some extra salad in case you were hungry. It's in the fridge.'

'Thank you.' His thoughtfulness touched her.

'Why not join me?'

Louise went through to the kitchen

and found the mixed salad he had arranged on a plate. She added some cottage cheese, then selected one of the granary rolls she had purchased earlier.

They had their meal at the table on one corner of the patio, shaded by trees and cooler now the sun had moved round. Although the air was still heavy, a gentle breeze had sprung up and the windchime tinkled faintly in the background.

Dan proved to be amusing company, and she soon relaxed. They talked about all manner of things, from her work to music, films to the wonders of Australia's Barrier Reef.

It wasn't until later that she realised he skilfully avoided revealing a single scrap of information about himself, whereas her life appeared to be an open book to him.

The week-end followed a similar pattern. True to his word, Dan was no trouble.

In fact, she hardly saw him, but she

discovered to her annoyance that out of sight in no way meant out of mind.

He went out a couple of times in his hire car, but he was never gone long, and she assumed he spent most of his time working on his mysterious research in his room.

On Saturday night, she went out to the theatre with Tony, a fellow teacher and a widower with whom she enjoyed companionable dinners and nights out, each of them safe in the knowledge that neither demanded too much. Each had memories of the past that guarded them from future commitments.

After spending most of Sunday in the garden, Louise arrived in the kitchen to discover Dan had whipped up a tempting cauliflower cheese which they enjoyed with crusty bread and a bottle of wine at the relatively cool patio table.

Louise watched him as he cleared his plate, marvelling that a man with such a hearty appetite should be so lean and fit.

His presence in the house had not been intrusive, and yet her awareness of him grew with each passing hour. The routine of having him around was becoming disconcertingly familiar.

Already she had begun to notice all kinds of things about him: that he wore his watch on his right wrist and was left-handed like her; that he had a faint scar across his chin that intrigued her, various mannerisms like the way he absently rubbed the tips of his right thumb and forefinger together when he was lost in thought.

She didn't want to notice things, didn't want him to impinge on her consciousness on a personal level. He was one more guest, and soon he would be gone.

★ ★ ★

By Monday, the electric tension that charged the air between them was beginning to affect her.

As Dan relaxed for an hour after

breakfast, sunbathing on the lawn, Louise found she was unable to settle to anything. After her gaze had strayed through her study window to where his recumbent form lounged on the grass for the tenth time in as many minutes, Louise thrust her chair back from the desk and stalked from the room.

Impatient with herself, she plunged into a bout of housework and had worked off some of her nervous energy by the time she had reached the upstairs. Her room finished, she manoeuvred the vacuum cleaner out on to the landing and decided to give Dan's room a quick once-over while he was otherwise occupied.

To her surprise, she discovered the door was locked. As she turned the handle once more, wondering if it was stuck, Dan's voice from behind her almost gave her heart failure.

'What are you doing?'

Cheeks glowing from her exertions coloured further with unnecessary guilt, as if she had been caught doing something she shouldn't.

'I didn't hear you come up,' she replied nervously. 'You startled me. I was just going to clean your room.'

Dan smoothly reversed their positions so that he placed himself between her and the door.

'There's no need for you to do that,' he stated, adjusting the T-shirt he had pulled on.

'But — '

'I thought guests lived as family.' He smiled, although his eyes remained watchful. 'Doesn't that extend to keeping their own rooms shipshape? Leave the cleaner there . . . I'll see to it.'

Louise stared at his closed expression. Short of having an all-out row, she could hardly force him to allow her the honour of cleaning his carpet. If he wanted to do it, that was fine with her.

'All right,' she conceded. 'I'll be out for a while, I have some errands to run in town.'

'See your later.'

She felt his gaze on her back as she walked down the landing to the stairs, and was halfway down before she heard the key in the lock of his door click open.

A frown creased her brow. Just what was Dan doing in there that he didn't want her to see? Her misgivings returned.

His manner had signified more than a normal desire for privacy — not that she was interested, exactly, but his furtiveness and the fact that he kept the door locked had roused her curiosity and her suspicions.

Concern nagged at her. Yes, he was charming and considerate, and he had not caused any trouble.

But what did she really know about him? Even, white teeth chewed at her lower lip. Just how close a friend was he of Greg's?

4

Louise was unable to pinpoint the precise moment she realised the man was following her. He had been in the library when she had returned some books, as he had been in the post office, the baker's, and now the chemist. Surely that was not pure chance?

A tingle of alarm travelled up her spine.

She had not caught him looking at her, but that made it more sinister somehow.

Unable to explain why, she kept her gaze averted, instinct telling her it was important he did not know she had discovered him.

Deliberately, she made a return visit to the post office, as if she had forgotten something.

As she waited with feigned idleness in the slow-moving queue, she glimpsed the man through the doorway. He was leaning against a shop-front across the street.

Louise took a deep breath.

No, it was not chance. For a moment, she wondered if she should go to the police, but what could she tell them that did not sound like she was being completely paranoid?

She thought of her car, parked in a multi-storey carpark, and wondered what she would do if he followed her in there. She had heard the horror stories and cursed herself for not listening to them. Why hadn't she found a place to park in the open?

The queue edged forward, and her gaze slid once more to the man who maintained his vigil across the road.

He was in his early twenties, looking like thousands of other young men in jeans and a T-shirt.

He had over-long blond hair that was scraped back from his brow, and his face was ordinary. In fact, he was the sort of person it would be impossible to describe to the police, she decided. He looked harmless, but appearances could be deceptive. He was following her, and she was not prepared to take any chances.

When she left the post office, she went to look round a large department store, and after a few moments of casual browsing, she ducked into a lift. She waited until all the people had vacated on the ground floor, then she took the lift up again to the floor she had just left. When the doors opened, the young man was nowhere in sight.

Louise breathed a sigh of relief. Her pulse was racing, her limbs shaking, and she wished she could believe the incident had been a figment of an over-active imagination.

She was unsure of her next move. She would have gone to the nearby antique shop run by her next-door neighbours for a reviving cup of tea and a consoling chat but Phillipa and Marcus were away until later in the week on a combined buying trip and holiday.

Having been anxious to escape the house, where one moment she was dangerously attracted to Dan and the next awash with suspicions about him, now all she wanted to do was return to its familiar sanctuary.

Louise made her way to the carpark at a brisk pace, her belief that she had shaken her stalker shattered when she saw him again, loitering in a stairway. She quickened her step.

The dark loneliness of the carpark brought a return of her anxieties. Her heart began to ricochet, the blood rushing in her veins, as she almost ran the last few yards to her car.

She fumbled with the keys, her fingers numb, dropping the key-ring twice before she was able to steady herself enough to open the door. Once inside the car, she slammed the door and secured the lock. The knot of fear tightened in her stomach. She forced herself to take several deep breaths.

With difficulty, she inserted the key in the ignition and offered up a prayer of thanks when the engine fired to life straight away.

As she drove jerkily away from the parking bay, she saw the shadow of a figure moving behind a concrete pillar. She kept her gaze averted and sped down the exit ramps, thankful when she was at last able to emerge on to the road and find sunlight and civilisation. But her relief was short-lived. She had not gone far when her slowing pulse began to race once more.

Was that motorbike several lengths back following her? The rider's face was obscured behind his helmet, but the figure was dressed in identical clothes to the man who had been following her in town.

It had to be a coincidence — didn't it? But the motorbike continued to tail her. As she neared the entrance to the private estate, she wondered if she should drive by, try to lose him. But she didn't have enough petrol for a jaunt round the countryside, and on reflection, it would be better to stay on familiar territory.

She thought longingly of the house. She would not be alone — Dan was there.

She swung off the road and on to the central avenue. In her rear-view mirror, she saw the bike come to a halt at the entrance, and the rider watched as she drove away.

That he knew where she lived alarmed her. He had not followed her farther, but he could be out there, watching, waiting for her to leave the house next time. And was watching all he was going to do? Did he have something more sinister in mind?

Shaking, Louise pulled the car to a shuddering halt in the drive and hurried for the house.

As soon as she walked into the hall, Dan could see how frightened she was. He had been on his way to the kitchen for a cold drink, but nothing was further from his mind now.

'What's happened?'

She stared at him, wide-eyed. He walked towards her, filled with a growing concern, and placed his hands on her shoulders. He could feel her body shaking.

'Louise,' he demanded. 'What's the matter?'

As she began to stumble over her story, anger welled inside him. Without conscious thought, he pulled her close and wrapped his arms around her in a hug of comfort.

At least, he had intended it would be a hug of comfort. Her nearness was playing havoc with his resolve. He felt her warm breath through the fabric of his shirt as she rested against him for a moment, and the lilac scent of her skin tormented him.

He drew back, and his hands cupped her face, his thumbs brushing away the trace of dampness that nestled beneath her eyes, eyes which held the lingering evidence of her fear.

He wanted to chase away that look of

fright. His gaze dropped to her parted lips. He wanted to still their tremble.

Unable to help himself, he bent his head and brushed his lips across hers in a gesture that was meant to be warm and reassuring. Meant to be. But it wasn't. From the first touch, he already felt out of control.

When he was finally able to make himself pull away, his every breath seared his lungs and his heart thudded against his ribs.

He looked at her flushed face, and those velvet-brown eyes were filled with a different kind of alarm, her lips trembling for a different reason — factors which were far too dangerous for his peace of mind. Shutting down his emotions, he stepped away from her.

'Stay inside and keep the door locked,' he instructed gruffly. 'I'll go down the road and take a look around.'

He heard her shut the door as he walked to his car. He revved the engine and reversed out of the drive, his actions betraying his inner turmoil.

Kissing her had been a stupid thing to do. He hadn't meant to, hadn't planned it, it had just happened.

And it shouldn't have. Thinking about her so much was turning his insides into knots.

He was playing with fire, in danger of losing his objectivity and messing up this job. Personalities had no place.

But she had looked so scared, and he had only wanted to do something to make her feel better. What a mess. He had made a huge mistake thinking he could keep at a distance. Against his will and his better judgment, Louise had crept under his skin.

She wasn't the most beautiful woman he had ever seen, but she had a loveliness that was more appealing, more dangerous, than surface beauty. She was serene, sensitive, graceful, intelligent . . . an English rose with her perfect complexion, her clear, guileless eyes, her mouth with its daring Cupid's bow. It was a package that threatened to make him lose his head.

Outwardly, she was so cool, and yet he sensed a fire simmering beneath the surface.

He wanted to fan those embers, light a touchpaper to the tinder of the passionate nature that he suspected she kept well hidden. He hadn't discovered why she hid it yet. And why was she hiding it? The idea intrigued him.

Dan grimaced. His English rose was 'way out of his league. He would be wise to remember their differences, the hundred different reasons why he should not become involved with her, why he had to resist the constant temptations she unconsciously set in his way.

For the first time he could ever remember, the solitary existence he had known for most of his life felt threatened.

Unable to recall leaving the estate, Dan drove along the main public road for a couple of miles, then pulled into a deserted layby. He took out his mobile phone and keyed in a number, drumming his fingers angrily on the steering wheel as he waited for his call to be answered.

'What kind of idiots are you employing?' he challenged with barely hidden fury once the connection was made. 'She spotted him following her — it frightened her half to death. You'll have to pull him off.'

Dan disconnected the call before his contact could give him a reply. He didn't like the way this was going one bit. Deep in thought, he put the car back into gear and turned in the direction of the house . . .

Once Dan had gone, Louise made her way to the kitchen on shaky legs and put the kettle on to boil. She raised unsteady fingers to her lips, still able to feel the imprint of his mouth on hers. The shock of his kiss had taken her breath away.

His gentleness had surprised her, his concern had warmed her, and his physical presence had made her feel safe. And his kiss? No, she didn't want to examine the effect that had on her.

She busied herself making tea and felt marginally better once she had drunk her first cup.

In no time at all, Dan was back, and she was thankful she had managed to take a grip on her scattered wits.

'Anything?' she asked anxiously as he came into the kitchen.

He shook his head, then helped himself to a cup of tea from the pot and sat at the table.

'I didn't imagine it, Dan, I — '

'I know. I believe you, Louise.'

He reached out and took her hand, enfolding it in his.

'But I assure you there is no-one there now.'

'Do you think I should call the police?'

He looked doubtful.

'Could you give them a full description, pick him out again?'

'I think so, but . . . '

She glanced at him and shrugged helplessly.

'There was nothing distinguishing about him.'

'Did you get the licence number of the motorbike?'

Louise shook her head glumly.

'Then I suggest you don't call them. I'm sure you'll find this was a one-off incident.'

'I hope so,' she exclaimed with an involuntary shiver.

'Nothing is going to happen to you while I'm here, I promise.'

Louise swallowed at the warm sincerity in his voice as he allayed her fears and made her feel protected.

'I'll stay with you. If we see him again, which I doubt we will, we'll get a good look at him, and go to the police together. Agreed?'

She nodded in confirmation, feeling the firmness of his touch as he squeezed her hand before he released her and moved away.

In bed that night, she tossed and turned, unable to sleep.

A combination of the oppressive heat and her thoughts about Dan compounded her restlessness, and she finally left her room and tiptoed downstairs.

She opened the patio doors hoping for any breath of air, then selected a favourite Cary Grant film and switched on the video. Cuddling a cushion to her chest, she sat on the settee in the dark to watch.

A few moments later, she heard Dan's footsteps in the hall, then his outline appeared silhouetted in the doorway.

'Are you OK?' he asked in tones that showed his concern.

'Yes.' She pressed the pause button. 'I just couldn't sleep.'

'What are you watching?'

He stepped into the room.

' 'Arsenic and Old Lace.' '

'Ah, a Cary Grant fan!'

She saw him smile in the darkness.

'Wait for me.'

He was back a few moments later and came across to sit beside her on the settee.

He handed her a spoon and set a tub of sinfully-delicious, hazelnut meringue ice cream between them.

Louise smiled to herself as they sat in companionable silence, the moon tracing a silvery path across the carpet as they watched the film and shared the ice cream.

'Feeling better?' Dan asked softly when the film had finished.

Louise switched off the television and stood up.

'Yes, thank you.'

She was surprised how comforting his presence had felt, and it had been kind of him to keep her company.

'Do you think you can sleep now?' he asked.

She nodded, a shiver running through her as he traced a gentle path down her cheek with the fingers of one hand.

'Then I'll see you in the morning.'

Louise went upstairs a few minutes after him, and as she slid back into bed, she drifted off to sleep with a smile on her face at his caring thoughtfulness.

* * *

Dan left the house after breakfast the following day, and Louise was contemplating which of the tasks that awaited her to tackle when the telephone rang.

'Ginny!' she exclaimed, surprised to hear her sister's voice. 'Is everything all right?'

'There's no need to worry, Louise, but — '

'What's wrong? Is it Mum?' she interrupted anxiously, fearing a recurring problem with the angina her mother suffered.

'She's all right, honestly. This afternoon she felt ill and had pains but the doctors are sure it's something she has eaten and not the angina at all.'

'Are you at the hospital?'

'Yes. Dad's with her, and she's already feeling better. They're going to keep her in overnight as a precaution, that's all.'

A nurse by training, Ginny was calm and unflappable, and Louise relaxed at the reassurance in her voice.

'You'll let me know if there's any other news?'

'Of course. I expect she'll ring herself in a day or so when we get back home.'

A note of excitement entered Ginny's voice.

'I have something else to tell you. I'm expecting another baby in February.'

'That's wonderful! How are you feeling?'

'Great. I hope the problems I had last time were the exception rather than the rule. I had no troubles with the first two pregnancies.'

Louise hesitated for a moment, then took the plunge.

'Is Greg there with you? Can I have a quick word?'

'Of course, I'll call him. I'll say goodbye and be in touch soon.'

Louise unconsciously chewed her bottom lip as she waited for her brother-in-law to come to the phone. Now she had the opportunity to ask about Dan, she was strangely reluctant.

'Hi,' Greg greeted, his voice as jaunty as ever. 'How's my favourite sister-in-law?'

'I'm fine. Congratulations, you rogue . . . more nappies!'

'Don't start on me already, Louise. Why not do the decent thing and come over to play the doting aunt? Help us out here!'

Louise laughed.

'By the way, I thought I told you I didn't want to have anyone to stay this summer,' she said.

'You did. I haven't forgotten.'

'And Daniel Kinsella?'

'Who?'

'Greg,' she protested, endeavouring to keep her voice light and hoping he wasn't serious.

'I've never heard of him.'

'But . . .'

Her voice trailed off and a cold shiver ran through her.

'Are you sure?'

A serious note appeared in Greg's voice.

'What's all this about, Louise?'

'He says you sent him.'

'Well, I didn't. You told him to get lost, yes?'

'Greg . . .'

'Are you all right? Is he at the house? I don't like this, Louise.'

She gulped.

She didn't like it either, but she did not want to alarm Greg or her family, especially at the moment.

'I expect I've got my wires crossed,' she improvised. 'I'll take care of it.'

'You're sure?'

'Absolutely.'

'If you need anything, or you want me to check it out, you get in touch,' he insisted. 'Promise? I'm only on the other end of the phone remember.'

'I promise. Thanks, Greg.'

Louise hung up a moment later and wrapped her arms around her waist. A lump of anxiety lodged in her throat and her chest felt tight.

Just who was Daniel Kinsella? Why was he here? If Greg had never heard of him, how did Dan know so much about her and her family?

5

It had been a frustrating morning and Dan had the feeling things weren't going to get any easier. He felt on edge when he arrived back at Louise's house and as soon as he went inside, he sensed a change in the atmosphere, a tension wholly different to the electric charge of attraction that had been growing between them.

'Louise?'

'I'm in the sitting-room.'

Dan frowned.

Her voice sounded odd — cool and stiff. He walked to the doorway and saw her standing by the ornate fireplace, her back ramrod straight. She had retreated back into her professional persona, the relaxed, tempting Louise hidden once more in businesslike clothes with those rich, red tresses restrained in a demure knot. He didn't like the change in her.

'What's wrong?'

'I spoke with Greg today.'

Her chin lifted, and she folded her arms across her chest.

'He's never heard of you.'

His expression never flickered as he held Louise's gaze, but he could see a welter of emotions chase through her deep brown eyes, ranging from concern and suspicion to anger and a smattering of alarm.

He moved slowly into the room and sat down a comfortable distance away from her. He hoped the position would make him appear less threatening and imposing.

He cursed to himself. Family contact had been a risk, but they had decided it was worth the gamble.

He had not imagined the deception would be discovered so soon. Now he had to think fast and minimise the danger.

His instincts told him to tell Louise the truth here and now, but he knew he couldn't do that. He hadn't always obeyed orders, far from it, but in this instance, he knew it would be best if explanations came from higher up.

The immediate problem was Louise herself.

He couldn't risk letting her out of his sight because he didn't know what she might do, and he couldn't allow her to jeopardise the operation.

She was irate, a bit scared, and that made her unpredictable. He couldn't take any chances.

His best option was to take her in. But how was he going to get her to go with him without frightening her any further? Clearly she was in no mood to trust him.

'Aren't you going to say anything?' she demanded, accusation and irritation in her voice. 'You don't know Greg, do you?'

'No.'

She took a deep breath.

'And you never had any kind of arrangement to stay here.'

'No.'

'I suppose you are going to tell me you can explain.'

'Yes.'

'I don't think I'm going to like it.'

'I'm sure you won't.'

A brief smile pulled the corners of his mouth.

'Try anyway.'

'I know you have no reason to trust me now,' he began, 'but I want to reassure you first of all that you are in no danger from me.'

Louise wanted to believe him. He had lied to her, yes, but he had given her no cause to fear him.

If he had wanted to harm her, there had been ample opportunity before now, and there was no reason why he should have waited until his trickery had been exposed?

But what did it all mean? What purpose could he have for cheating his way into her house?

'I'm waiting,' she pressed, prepared to hear him out.

'I have to ask you to bear with me a

little longer. I want you to come with me to town.'

'Why?'

She eyed him warily.

'I'll explain when we get there.'

'Why can't you explain here?'

'Please,' he persisted, his eyes sincere and unwavering. 'There is a reason, Louise.'

She couldn't explain, even to herself, why she allowed him to sweet-talk her round to agreeing to go with him, but less than half an hour later, he was parking his car outside a converted office building in the town centre.

He opened the car door for her and waited for her to get out, then ushered her across the pavement.

Louise stared at the building with its crumbling plaster and peeling paint. Why had Dan brought her here?

Fresh anxiety nibbled at her, and she stiffened as his hand at the small of her back guided her to the entrance of what had once been a large, end-of-terrace house.

Inside, the passage was drab and unwelcoming, with patches of damp on the outside wall. A musty air of neglect prevailed. Ahead of her was a flight of bare wooden stairs, and after a moment of hesitation, she allowed Dan to escort her up.

The flight of stairs took a half turn, and at the top was a solid door, from behind which came the sounds of a typewriter, the murmur of voices and the ringing of a telephone.

Dan opened the door and encouraged her inside.

The jumbled office looked as if it had been hastily put together. Louise frowned.

Half a dozen people were at work in the main room, but the activity and hum of conversation ceased for an instant when she and Dan walked in. She was uncomfortably aware that she had become the centre of attention, that curious gazes rested on her.

They appeared — what? Louise searched for the right word and realised that shocked came readily to mind.

She glanced at Dan. He had made eye-contact with a woman who sat at a computer screen nearby, and as if in answer to a silent question, he shrugged his shoulders.

'Kinsella!'

Louise jumped as the angry voice boomed across the room, and she saw a bald, older man framed imposingly in the doorway of a glass-partitioned office.

'In here, now.'

Beside her, she could feel Dan tense but the smile he gave her was one of encouragement.

He sat her down on a vacant chair, and Louise watched as he walked into the office and closed the door.

Louise was confused and wary, and she wanted to know what was going on. As she waited impatiently, she could see Dan arguing with the man in the office. Once or twice, they glanced at her, but they appeared no nearer an agreement, and Louise couldn't make out what they were discussing so heatedly.

She started in surprise when a bearded man of indeterminate age handed her a polystyrene cup of coffee.

'Thank you,' she murmured, but the man merely nodded and moved back to his desk.

Just when the tension was beginning to drive her to the point of explosion, the office door opened and Dan gestured for her to enter.

Nervously, Louise set her untouched cup of coffee aside and walked slowly to the office.

The man who sat behind the paper-strewn desk rose as she went in.

Louise discovered he was even more disconcerting close to. His face was weathered, and his eyes, watchful chips of blue ice, crinkled to slits as he gave a semblance of a smile in greeting.

There was an almost stifling heat in his office. A fan on top of a filing cabinet stirred some papers and a couple of large photographs lay turned face down on the desk.

Louise flicked a hasty glance at Dan who had taken up a position leaning nonchalantly against the windowsill.

The man behind the desk extended his hand, and Louise switched the focus of her attention back to him.

She accepted the gesture warily.

'Please sit down, Miss Shepherd,' he invited with a voice that rasped like coarse gravel. 'We won't delay you longer than necessary.'

Louise sat down, conscious of Dan's gaze on her. She watched as the older man took a wallet from a pocket of his jacket that hung on the back of his chair. He flipped it open and handed it to her.

'My name is Norman Curry. Here is my identification.'

As she took the leather wallet, she met the icy, blue stare, then she glanced down.

Her eyes widened in astonishment as she looked at his photograph and the official badge the wallet contained.

Her gaze shot back to his.

'You're a policeman?'

'Of a sort, yes.'

'Why am I here?' she demanded, disconcerted by the turn of events.

Norman Curry returned the wallet to his jacket pocket and regarded her for a moment in frowning consideration.

'How well do you know your neighbours, Miss Shepherd?'

The unexpectedness of the question took Louise very much by surprise.

'I beg your pardon?'

'Marcus and Phillipa Whitehead. How well do you know them?'

'We're friends. We see each other for dinner, pop in for a drink, visit the theatre occasionally, that kind of thing,' she explained in confusion, intimidated by the cold, blue stare. 'Why are you asking me these questions?'

Norman Curry showed no inclination that he intended to answer her query.

'Have you ever met a man at their house by the name of Ramon, Miguel Ramon — heavy build, dark, foreign?'

'No,' she answered, her concern increasing as the interrogation continued. 'I've never seen him, or heard of him.'

His brow drawn in a scowling frown, Norman Curry leaned back in his chair and watched her for a moment before speaking again.

'Miss Shepherd, my information shows me that you are a woman of high character, and while it is somewhat irregular, I must take you into my confidence because I need your co-operation.'

'I don't understand.'

'Miguel Ramon is wanted in several countries for his involvement in money-laundering and drug-trafficking activities. Our inquiries give us reason to believe that the Whiteheads have become involved with this man through their antique business, that they are somehow implicated in his criminal enterprise. We — '

'But that's ridiculous,' Louise interrupted, unable to listen to any more of this far-fetched explanation.

She turned her appalled gaze towards Dan but could read nothing of his thoughts.

'They are just an ordinary couple. There must be some mistake.'

'The facts speak for themselves.'

Louise met Norman Curry's implacable gaze.

'If what you are telling me is true, what do you want of me?'

'The Whiteheads have only come to our attention recently, and we know little about them. Living where you do, it has been . . . difficult to carry out necessary observations in the usual way.'

'You are saying you need to use my house to spy on my friends,' she riposted bluntly.

'If you wanted my co-operation why not ask me? Why gain entry under false pretences?'

Her queries were met with a drawn-out silence as both men exchanged glances.

Louise's indignation increased with a

flash of understanding.

'You thought I was involved?'

'It was a possibility we couldn't ignore,' Norman Curry pointed out.

Louise was in no way mollified. She turned accusing eyes to Dan who met her gaze unflinchingly.

'Can I assume I am no longer under suspicion?' she challenged, sarcasm in her tone.

'That is so, Miss Shepherd.'

Norman Curry sighed and sat forward, resting his arm on the desk.

'I appreciate this is difficult for you, and I realise that helping us may not seem appealing to you, but I must still request your assistance.'

Louise sent him a derisive glare.

'Request? I can refuse?'

'I trust you won't,' he intoned with a thin smile.

Before Louise could make further comment, there was a knock on the door, and the man who had brought her coffee stepped inside.

'Dan, customs at Heathrow are on

the phone. I think you should talk to them.'

'All right.'

He nodded towards Norman Curry then hesitated briefly by Louise's chair but left the room without looking at her.

'Excuse me,' he said.

'Miss Shepherd, what these people are doing is dangerous and immoral. You are a teacher, you know how impressionable your students are and I am sure you would not sleep at night with the knowledge people who could supply them with drugs, ruin their futures, were not apprehended.'

Louise held his stare, annoyed at the emotional blackmail.

'If you know so much about their activities, why not arrest them now?'

'Our evidence in court must be iron-clad, and we want all those involved in the net when we close it — the big fish as well as the minnows.'

'And if I agree, what do you expect of me?'

'That Kinsella remains in your house, and is able to carry out the job he has been assigned. His methods are up to him, and he may request that you arrange an introduction, but that is something you must discuss with him as the circumstances warrant.'

Louise was silent as she absorbed Norman Curry's words.

His veiled threat concerning the effects drugs could have had hit home. She knew she would never forgive herself if her hesitation and obstruction had allowed anyone involved in supplying them to remain free. But it was all so much to take in at once.

'If it wasn't vitally important and if we could carry out the necessary surveillance another way, we would not involve you.'

'All right,' she conceded. 'I'll do as you ask.'

'I'm glad we understand each other.'

Louise was unable to return his smile.

'May I ask how long Dan will be in my house?'

'Only as long as it takes to get the information we need. It's hard to say exactly. A week, maybe two.'

A flash of enmity in his eyes surprised her.

'Kinsella is a maverick, unorthodox, but he knows his job, Miss Shepherd.'

The interview over, Norman Curry rose and shook her hand before he showed her out of his office.

Louise saw Dan talking with a couple of men at a desk nearby, but she stalked past him towards the exit.

He caught her up at the door.

'Louise . . . '

She ignored him and started down the staircase, only to pull up short with a gasp of recognition.

In the hallway below, a young man had just come through the entrance — a young man dressed in casual clothes, his blond hair scraped back from his face. It was the same man who had followed her in town.

'I was going to tell you,' Dan began, but she shook off his restraining hand.

Her anger rose as she continued down the stairs.

Angry brown eyes met the embarrassed apology in the young man's grey gaze, but she was in no mood for understanding or forgiveness. Once out in the street, she dragged warm air into her lungs and waited impatiently by the car. The sooner she was away from this place the better.

Dan had lied to her, used her. She wished she never had to see him again.

6

'Louise, please, I think we should talk about this. There must be loads of things you want to ask me about all this.'

Dan spoke to her softly as he followed her into the house a short time later but she kept her back to him as she walked towards her study.

'I don't want to talk to you.'

She closed the door and locked it.

She had never been so angry. The journey back to the house had been completed in stony silence, and if she had to see or talk to Dan any time soon, she wasn't sure what she might do.

For several minutes, she paced up and down the room, her mind buzzing with all that had taken place over the last hours.

Not only had Dan deceived her from

the first moment, but if what Norman Curry had told her was true, then the neighbours she had looked on as friends for the last couple of years had betrayed that friendship.

It hurt. She had trusted them, shared things with them, given them her confidence.

However much she wished otherwise, she could not believe Norman Curry and his unit would reach this stage of an investigation if the case against Phillipa and Marcus was not a strong one.

She just couldn't believe her friends were different from who and what they had appeared.

How could it be true?

Louise slumped on her chair, and, elbows propped on the desk, she covered her face with her hands.

Traitorously, her thoughts turned to Dan. He was the traitor — and that fact hurt just as much.

She realised now why he had been adamant about occupying that particular room. It was the only one in the house that afforded a view over the Whiteheads' property.

It was also clear why he had not wanted her to go into his room.

But it was the chance encounter with the man who had followed her that upset her the most.

She had been scared at the time. Dan had known the truth and had still allowed her to believe she had been stalked.

He had glossed it over with a veneer of concern and understanding, going out of his way to be solicitous and comforting, but he had known.

No wonder he had skilfully sown doubts and dissuaded her from calling the police. How he must have laughed at her. She had been so stupid.

And he was still here, under her roof for the foreseeable future — and however much Norman Curry had dressed it up in polite requests, she had not really been given a choice.

Somehow, she had to find a way to

live with Dan's presence, a way that guarded her from the effect he had on her.

She knew she was vulnerable to him. The last few days had proved that beyond doubt.

Dan sat in the kitchen, ignoring the tea he had recently made, a dark frown on his face.

He knew Louise needed time to come to terms with what had happened but he wished she would talk about it so they could clear the air.

She was angry, that was obvious, and she had every right to be.

Despite the reason that had brought it about, it was good to see her lose that cool reserve she maintained, and being passionate about something.

But he had to stop thinking about her. There was no way a woman like her would have anything to do with a man like him, even if the circumstances of their meeting had been different.

And unless this situation had been different, they would never have met at all. They came from opposite worlds.

His head told him to respect the status quo and maintain this new distance between them.

Other than on a professional basis when contact between them was necessary to establish his cover with the Whiteheads, he and Louise should keep well away from each other.

That's what his head told him.

But he didn't want to do that. He didn't want to keep that distance between them, to hide from the electric attraction that refused to be displaced by anger or distrust.

He wanted to be with her, to listen to her laugh, to touch her, to kiss her — all the things that weren't sensible.

There was no future in it, there could be nothing between them. But he still couldn't stop himself from wanting so much.

When this was over — the thought trailed off, and he tipped his chair back, balancing it on two legs, his grim expression reflecting his inner turmoil.

When it was over, Louise would be glad to banish him from her life and he would walk away and move on to the next case.

But while he was here, he didn't think he could resist unravelling the hidden Louise, the one he had only glimpsed so far.

When Louise finally came into the kitchen, Dan turned from the worktop where he was making a salad for supper and watched her.

He hated to see the dull resignation and distrust in her eyes as she glanced at him then hastily turned away. It made him feel like a completely worthless human being. In silence, she crossed the kitchen and poured herself a glass of milk. She stood with her back to him.

Her carriage was stiff, as she gazed out of the window in the direction of the rose-covered arch, heavy with scented bloom, that separated the end of the drive from the side entrance to the garden.

'The airport hire car was a nice

touch,' she remarked, a cool edge of bitterness in her tone as her voice slashed the tense silence. 'You certainly thought of everything.'

'Louise,' he began placatingly, but his words faltered as she turned to face him.

Dan could sense the anger that still simmered deep within her. If anger had been the only thing, he could have dealt with it.

But her cheeks were pale, the deep, brown eyes awash with hurt and combined with the sense of something lost that had crept into her voice, his gut wrenched in response.

His hands curled to fists by his sides.

Every instinct screamed at him to go to her and take her in his arms but he knew it was too soon.

'You should have been an actor, Dan. You played your part to perfection,' she praised with forced lightness as she sat down at the table. 'I'll have to get you to come and give some tips to my drama class.'

However much he deserved them, her words hurt.

He couldn't explain to her how much it had pained him to deceive her, because that would mean admitting, to himself as well as her, just how deeply he felt.

He wasn't ready to do that — he didn't know if he would ever be ready.

As difficult as it was, he forced thoughts of Louise to the back of his mind and tried to be businesslike and professional.

'We need to discuss what's happened and where we go from here. I have a job to do, and while I'm here, it will be easier for both of us if you give me your co-operation.'

'Nothing about this will make it easier for me. But,' she added with a derisive smile, 'anything that will speed the end of this unsavoury business is fine with me.'

Dan swallowed a fresh wave of hurt at her cool reserve and distant manner. What else could he expect after all that had happened? He pulled out a chair and sat opposite her.

'I can't change the past, Louise, no matter how much I may wish to. I did what was necessary, what I was briefed to do.'

'Is that meant to make me feel better?'

'No.'

He sighed and ran his fingers through his hair.

'We should clear the air. If there are things you want to know, ask me, and if I can answer, I will. Then we can decide how best to handle the next couple of weeks.'

Louise decided he looked sincere but then he had appeared that way before. She wasn't sure how she could ever trust him again.

'You lied to me.'

'Yes.'

'And you'll do it again.'

She saw his eyes cloud as he looked at her.

'Not if I can help it.'

Louise did not think that was a satisfactory answer but she decided not to push it.

He would only tell her what he wanted to, after all, and how could she know if what he said was true or false?

Her thoughts slipped back to the day he had arrived, that weird feeling she'd experienced that Dan had searched the house. Her gaze met his, but the question remained unasked. She knew the answer now, but she did not want to hear the words out loud.

'There's a file of information about me?'

Dan nodded in response but remained silent.

Clearly she had been investigated, and she felt exposed, violated, at the invasion of her privacy. Dan had taken over her house, her life, knew things about her he had no right to know.

'What does your file say?' she asked.

'Norman Curry's file, not mine,' he corrected calmly.

Louise shrugged at the subtle difference.

'But you've seen it.'

'Yes.' He watched her, his mouth set in that characteristic pout of consideration she was coming to know so well. 'General things, home, family, job. I know you were almost married three years ago but you didn't go through with it, that you changed your job and moved back here.'

There was a questioning note in his voice but Louise had no intention of filling in the details of that time in her life for him.

Discovering Julian's unfaithfulness and indiscretions had been a vicious blow, especially coming as it did a mere fortnight before the wedding.

Aside from the embarrassment of cancelling the arrangements, making excuses, sending back the presents that had arrived, there had been the hurt, disappointment and sense of betrayal to overcome. It had been so painful to see all her dreams turn to ashes.

She had picked the wrong time to challenge Julian. He had been worse for drink, and in the blazing row that had followed, he had hit her — hard. It had only happened once, but she was not foolish enough to imagine it wouldn't happen again. A leopard never changed its spots.

Not prepared to listen to his half-hearted apologies, she had left, not about to subject herself to a repeat performance.

At least she had discovered the truth before they were married, not afterwards.

But not before the substantial balance of the savings account had been cleared. Besotted, she had seen no reason to doubt their love or their future together, and she had been grossly naïve in allowing Julian to sweet-talk her misgivings away.

But he had swept aside her initial doubts and the account had been in his name only.

She had no idea where he had gone.

It had been a painful and expensive lesson but one she had learned well.

Louise glanced at Dan and saw him regarding her changing expressions intently.

She had already been mixed up with one lying, cheating man and she had no intention of ever trusting another one.

'None of what you have uncovered of my past has any bearing on the matter at hand,' she said now, her voice stiff and cool. 'As a point of interest, has anything you ever told me been the truth?'

'Everything I told you about me.'

'Which isn't much. You are very clever at avoiding questions, aren't you?'

She paused and offered a grim smile when he failed to respond.

'See what I mean? I suppose the less you say and the closer you stick to the truth, the less likely you are to trip yourself up, in your line of work I mean.'

'Something like that.' Dan did not flinch.

'And speaking of your work . . . imports and exports, wasn't it?'

'Based on fact,' he insisted. 'Only not in the sense I implied it, but in trying to stop illegal ones.'

With reluctance, Louise conceded the point.

The man had an answer for everything, and it was a waste of time trying to match wits with him.

'Are you really Australian, or English?'

'Both.'

Louise raised her eyebrows, her voice a sarcastic murmur.

'How clever of you.'

'I was born here,' he explained, then hesitated almost imperceptibly before he continued.

'My parents moved to Hong Kong when I was six, then to Australia when I was nine. I was sent back to school here in England.'

Sensing a hidden tension in him, Louise remained silent. Although she was anxious for him to continue, wanting to learn more about him in spite of herself, she knew if she pushed him he would clam up.

So she waited, watching the hardening of his expression from beneath her lashes.

'I was a product of your fancy private school system until I was sixteen. I've spent the last sixteen years running away from it.'

Louise couldn't imagine Dan running from anything, but to give lie to her, he rose from the table to evade her searching gaze and returned to finish preparing the salad.

For some moments, she thought he wasn't going to tell her any more but at last he spoke again, a cold tightness in his voice that spoke of his inner pain.

'I never stood a chance of fitting in. My father had come from what's known as the working classes. He was new money, wanting to be old, so he sent me to a school with boys from families who could trace their titled ancestry back for centuries, because it looked good for him. I hated it but when did my feelings ever count for anything?'

She ached for the hurt, lonely, little boy the man could not hide even all these years later. But she doubted he would thank her for an expression of sympathy or compassion, so she held her tongue and waited for him to continue.

'The older I got, the worse it became. I loved my holidays in Australia, the friends I made there, and I wanted to stay, to be like them, but it was no use. And so I rebelled — against the restrictions placed on me, the way of life, the people who were so different from me, my family.'

'That's understandable.'

Dan threw an ironic glance over his shoulder.

'I was something of a hellion, hated by the boys at school, not accepted by their families — and not accepted by my own father because I could never be what he wanted me to be.'

'Parental disapproval and interference has no class barrier, Dan.'

'Maybe not.' He shrugged. 'But my 'lack of social standing and breeding, and my father's own designs above his station' had their affect on me. That was a quote, by the way.'

Louise frowned, disconcerted by this problem he seemed to have with money and class.

'What happened?'

'I scraped through my exams and went back to Sydney at the end of the final term. I refused to fall in with my father's future plans for me and that led to a huge row.'

A rift it seemed that had never been healed.

'And then?' she prompted softly, leaning forward to rest her arms on the table.

'My father kicked me out. I hung around for a while, did some really stupid things, got into a lot of strife. One man, Craig Slater, a police sergeant, saw past the bad-boy image to some good inside. I sure as hell didn't know it was there,' he admitted, turning to set two plates of salad on the table. 'He helped me turn my life around. I reckon he saved my life, Louise.'

She nodded her understanding, trying to imagine what his life must have been like growing up in such an environment.

'How old were you then?'

'Nineteen.'

Dan took a jug of iced water from the fridge and set it on the table, then added a basket of crusty rolls, some butter, and finally the cutlery.

'Thank you,' she smiled at him, forgetting she was supposed to be angry and uncomfortable with him.

'Wasn't it something of a jump from law breaker to law enforcer?'

Dan returned the smile, his eyes less troubled than before.

'Yeah, but Craig persuaded me I could do more to help other kids like me from the inside of the system rather than the outside. A lot of things he said made sense. It took a while but I straightened myself out and with Craig's help I finally joined the police.'

'In Sydney?' she asked, helping herself to a roll and breaking through the crispy crust.

'Right. I went through various departments and ended up displaying a surprising talent for special investigations.'

Louise hid a smile at the note of discomfort in his voice as he spoke the words.

'So how come you've ended up with some special breakaway investigations unit in England?'

Dan went completely still, and slowly raised his gaze to hers.

She saw his eyes cloud and fill with cold, dark shadows. She felt suddenly afraid.

'While working on an unrelated investigation, I uncovered the evidence of my father's fraudulent past that helped to put him in prison.'

7

After Dan had dropped his bombshell, the kitchen suddenly became unnaturally quiet. Louise stared at him, her fork suspended in mid-air on its journey to her mouth.

With infinite care, she lowered it back to her plate. He withdrew his gaze from hers, his mouth a tight line, a dark frown between his brows, and returned his concentration to his meal. But he wasn't eating, just pushing the food around with his fork.

Louise began to think.

How best could she draw him out? She sensed it was unusual for him to talk about himself, that perhaps he needed to but if he had time to think about it he would stop.

'What happened, Dan?'

He raised his gaze and she saw a mix of confusion and hurt in his eyes along with indecision.

'I did a lot of soul-searching, unsure what to do with the information I had uncovered but family or not, in the end I passed it on.'

Louise nodded in encouragement when he paused again, looking at her as if to detect some sign of admonishment at what he had done. She knew he would not find any.

'It was devastating to discover what my father had done — and later to learn that it was not the first time.'

He pushed his plate aside and propped his elbows on the table.

'It turned out that my father's business in Australia had been founded on money fraudulently obtained while he was working in Hong Kong. That dirty money paid for my expensive education. All I ever wanted was a normal childhood and some basic family life.'

Dan poured himself a glass of water and took a long swallow.

'And your mother?'

'She blamed me, said I had made their lives hell, ruined their future by what I did,' he retorted, the anger in his voice failing to mask the pain. 'What about the lives he ruined, cheating and swindling people out of their savings? Despite having all that money, it still wasn't enough and after some years working in his legitimate business in Australia, he started up another scam.'

'How long ago did you find out?'

Dan leaned back in his chair, his gaze hooded.

'Six years. I haven't seen or spoken with either of my parents since.'

Louise felt sad for him.

She imagined his childhood — banished from the family home, his adolescence — when he was desperate for love and acceptance and not finding anything he needed.

It explained a great deal about the man he had become.

Was his very job, investigating and apprehending others guilty of criminal activities some kind of crusade, a way of punishing his own father?

She looked at him intently.

It was a new side to him she had discovered today, one that showed his toughness was only surface deep.

Hidden below, there lurked an unexpected vulnerability. Louise recognised that it made him more dangerous to her peace of mind.

Wanting to offer him some understanding and support, she pushed her own forgotten meal aside and leaned closer to him, her voice soft.

'Dan, you did the right thing, the only thing you could have done.'

'Did I, Louise?'

The troubled eyes stared back at her.

'You see, I don't think I'll ever know why I did it. Was it for justice, for the sake of the people whose lives he had made a misery, because I couldn't let a guilty man go free? Or was it something less altruistic, more fundamental . . . unconscious revenge against the father who had never shown me any love or understanding?'

Frowning, Louise watched as he pushed back his chair and stood up. He turned away and walked out of the room, his body stiff with tension. Getting slowly to her feet, Louise crossed the kitchen and began to make coffee, her mind full of what he had told her.

Perhaps this was the first real truth he had shared, the first thing that had come straight from his heart.

She could understand his concerns but knew he'd had no choice, whatever his inner reasons had been. She hoped he would see that and would one day forgive himself.

She could also understand his need to get away and make a fresh start amongst people who knew nothing of what had happened. Hadn't she felt the same after Julian?

All of which came back to the fact that Daniel was here, in her house, investigating Marcus and Phillipa who had lied to her and betrayed her trust. She realised now that Dan would understand the mental turmoil she was experiencing.

Dan himself had deceived her and she didn't like it, but she would make the best of the situation and not put obstacles in his way.

Her decision made, she took down two cups and saucers and poured the fresh coffee.

★ ★ ★

Dan wandered about the garden, the heat still thick in the air, a knot of annoyance pulling his brows together. He had never talked to another living soul as he had just talked to Louise, not even in the old days with Craig Slater.

He had certainly never shared his feelings, talked of his past, his childhood, his father.

So why had he opened up to Louise? He didn't like it and didn't want to speculate on the reasons why he was vulnerable to her.

When she stepped out on to the patio and set two cups and saucers on the table, he eyed her warily.

Reluctantly, he strolled across the sunbaked lawn and sat down, accepting his coffee with a nod of appreciation.

'What do you want me to do?'

The softly-spoken question surprised him, and he glanced at her, finding none of the former anger.

What had changed her mind? He took a sip of his coffee, plans formulating in his head.

'Tell me everything you know about the Whiteheads.'

★ ★ ★

He listened as she talked, storing away any scrap of information that could be useful to the investigation or assist in obtaining evidence.

He felt her hurt at the sense of betrayal and wished he could ease it for her but he held his tongue, keeping off any personal issues. Occasionally he asked a question, clarified a point, and it was dusk by the time Louise had told him all she could.

'How long have you been working on this?' she asked, turning her empty cup in her hands.

'Personally, a few months, but the unit has been after Ramon for some time.'

He looked at her, wondering just how much he could tell her about the case. He figured she had a right to know the basics, at least, so long as it didn't compromise the investigation.

Dan turned his chair and propped his feet on the seat of an empty one across from him.

'Ramon is slippery as an eel. He's clever, too, careful to divide things up, spread information and money and drugs around so that no-one place has too much, no one person knows too much.

'It was a fluke the connection with

the Whiteheads was discovered but almost at once, things began to fall into place. For the first time there is a light at the end of the tunnel, a real chance we can get him.'

'And Phillipa is really involved? She's not just an innocent bystander in this?'

Dan hated to hurt her, but knew she needed the truth from him now.

'I'm sorry.'

'What have they done? How are they involved with this Ramon?'

'I can't tell you too much, Louise. Not because I don't want to, but because I really can't, and anyway, it will be better for you. Less chance of giving anything away.'

'I see.'

'All I can say is they are involved in laundering the drug money through their antiques business and transporting packages on trips abroad.'

He paused for a moment, then added, 'There are a string of safe deposit boxes for drops, and a couple of bank accounts in Zurich.'

Dan watched as Louise rose to her feet and paced across the patio. She wrapped her arms around her waist.

Shadowed in the early evening light, she was lovely, ethereal, graceful. With an effort, Dan tore his gaze away.

'You say they're due back from their trip tomorrow?' he asked, his voice more brusque than he had intended.

Louise nodded silently.

'It's important you help me to get inside the house.'

'Then what?' she questioned, turning to look at him.

'You leave me to worry about that.'

He saw her frown, hesitating before she spoke.

'It's Phillipa's birthday on Saturday, and they are having a party. I've been invited, but — '

'Perfect. We'll go together.'

'Together?'

'But I need a good cover to convince them I'm all right,' he explained, hiding a sudden smile.

Louise moved back towards him and

he could see the wariness on her face.

'What sort of cover do you have in mind?'

Dan linked his hands behind his head and regarded her with lazy speculation.

'The story is that we met in Australia when you were with your family last Christmas. We parted on a sour note and — '

'What?'

'And now I've come over to visit you,' he continued, ignoring her shocked interruption. 'We're giving it another try.'

'Giving what another try?'

This time, Dan could not stop the smile.

'Us.'

In the short silence that followed, Louise stared at him in horror. He couldn't be serious.

She swallowed a sudden restriction in her throat and struggled to find her voice.

'You mean you want them to think

that you and I were once together
. . . That we are . . . '

Her words faltered and trailed off.

'A couple,' Dan finished for her with underlying humour.

'No! I won't do it, absolutely not. And no-one would believe it, it's so ridiculous,' she floundered helplessly.

She saw Dan's eyes narrow to slits at her stream of protests.

'Why? Because I'm not on the same social plane as you?' he demanded, his voice harsh.

'That's not what I meant at all.'

'No?'

Stunned, Louise decided to ignore his challenge.

He was sensitive about his past, the way others had treated him but clearly he still had a chip on his shoulder about the whole business.

'Look,' she explained calmly, 'I meant that they will wonder why I have never mentioned you. They know I've been seeing Anthony, and expect me to go to the party with him.

Besides, it will be obvious we don't get along so why would they believe we are a couple?'

To her alarm, he rose to his feet and began to walk slowly across to her.

'Then we'll just have to work hard to convince them.'

'What do you mean?' she asked with dread, a split second before realisation set in and panicked her. 'No!'

Her lips felt inexplicably dry. Before she had the presence of mind to evade him, he cupped her chin with one hand and tilted her face towards his. His voice dropped to a husky whisper.

'I suggest we practise.'

'No!' she repeated.

Both her hands rose, her fingers locking around his wrist in a futile attempt to break his hold.

Instead, he increased the pressure and drew her inexorably closer, his touch firm but gentle.

Dan's lips brushed softly, teasingly, against hers. Louise drew in a breath and stifled an involuntary whimper before it could escape.

'Don't . . . '

'I can't help myself.'

His words breathed softly against her parted mouth, so quietly she almost missed them.

But she had no time to reflect because his lips slanted to seal hers in a passionate kiss that robbed her body of all thought and strength.

A rush of heat flooded through her as he pulled her roughly against him, and her arms stole around him of their own volition.

The potency of her sudden desire frightened her, and she struggled against him, dragging lungfuls of air when he raised his head a few inches and looked down at her.

'If teachers had looked like you when I was at school, I think I would have paid a lot more attention.'

'I'm sorry, Dan. This is a mistake. I'm not interested.'

'Are you sure about that, Louise?'

She watched Dan walk away and

disappear into the house, his mocking taunt ringing in her ears. How could she possibly ignore him?

He was getting to her. Her fingers lifted to press against her moist, trembling lips.

It was all a game to him, a means of passing the time while he was in her home.

But it was a game she could not afford to play.

* * *

She did not see Dan again that evening, and she told herself she was relieved.

After locking the house, she had a bath, then went to bed only to lie awake, unable to sleep.

She was all too aware of her passionate nature. It had landed her in the mess with Julian and since her break up with him, she had kept that side of her suppressed.

For those three years, she had managed to convince herself she neither needed nor missed a close, loving relationship in her life, while her friends and Anthony kept her intellectual and social lives stimulated and her job was engrossing and tiring.

Until Dan.

Louise sighed and turned her pillow over, searching for a cool patch. In a matter of days, Dan had made her realise all too clearly that her passionate self was not dead, only dormant.

Slowly but surely, he was bringing her back to life like the sun opening a flower.

She knew it was not sensible to allow him to do it, she just didn't know how to stop him.

She frowned into the darkness. It was the thing that was said about her most often; that she was sensible. The sensible girl had become a sensible woman. She had chosen a sensible career, lived a sensible life, had sensible relations, sensible friends.

There were times when she was fed up with being sensible, times when, even once, she would love to do something unpredictable, outrageous, irresponsible.

Not that there was anything the matter with being sensible, reliable, dependable, she assured herself, it just sounded so dull. Her life was ordered, planned, predictable, safe.

It was Dan's fault she was thinking like this. He had rocked her world to its foundations.

There was a wildness about him, a rough edge, the hint of something dangerous that was at once exciting yet frightening. Beneath the surface, there lurked turbulent emotions and fiery passions.

Anthony, on the other hand, was like her.

They shared the same careers, the same interests, the same reluctance to enter into any serious involvement. Their evenings out were to the theatre, a good restaurant, concerts. Sensible things.

She tried to imagine Dan sitting

peacefully through a Mozart recital and couldn't.

An evening with him would be more vital, more impulsive, more physical. Louise swallowed and tried to ignore the sudden hastening of her pulse. Her imagination was running away with itself again.

There was no doubt about it.

Dan Kinsella was a dangerous man. A self-mocking smile crossed her lips. She would do the sensible thing and ride out the storm until he departed from her life.

★ ★ ★

Dan lay in bed and stared at the ceiling, unable to sleep.

He had nearly lost it earlier on, nearly allowed his emotions to overrule his commonsense.

Hadn't he already told himself a hundred times to leave her alone? Angrily, he thrust his hands through his tousled hair, threw off the sheet and walked to the window.

The Whiteheads' house was in darkness but tomorrow they should be home, and then the really serious part of this operation would begin — an operation which, thanks to his sudden brainstorm this evening, now involved him more deeply with Louise.

It wasn't fair to use her. No matter how many times he told himself he was just doing his job, that her giving him cover was his best way in and out as quickly and efficiently as possible, he knew deep down it was an excuse to be with her.

What the hell was he doing? This house was professionally decorated and filled with old paintings and antique furniture.

Louise was so obviously different to him. His whole background was a sham, founded on lies.

He shouldn't mess her around or involve her any more deeply in the investigation. Anything that happened between them on a personal level could only be a short-term thing — and he cared too much about her to do that and then walk away.

There, now he had said it. His job carried risks, and he often had to bluff his way out of unexpected and difficult situations. But none of his training, in Australia, England, or on exchange with the FBI in Quantico, Virginia, was a scrap of use to him in this situation.

Because he had fallen for Louise Shepherd, and he had no idea what he was going to do about it.

8

I don't think I can do this,' Louise whispered as they stood on the doorstep of the Whiteheads' house on Saturday night.

'Yes, you can.'

Dan gave her hand a reassuring squeeze.

'Once you get started, it won't be so bad. I'll be with you.'

Louise wasn't sure if that was comforting or not. The last couple of days had been tense and they had circled each other warily. The atmosphere in the house had been charged with electricity, snapping and crackling until Louise's nerves became frazzled.

The prospect of this evening did not help.

Butterflies fluttered in her stomach and she felt on edge, anxious she did not make a mistake and nervous about facing Phillipa and Marcus now she knew what she did about them.

'Did I tell you how stunning you look?' Dan asked, his voice a husky murmur near her ear.

Louise shook her head, her skin tingling from the feel of his warm breath. He didn't look so bad himself, she allowed, but she had no intention of admitting it to him.

'Well, you do. The colour of that dress suits you perfectly.'

She felt herself growing hot at his words and his nearness.

'Thank you.'

She almost wished the door would hurry up and open and the crowd inside, whose cars lined the drive, would rescue her from the intimacy of being alone with Dan.

As if in response to her silent entreaty, the door at once swung open. Phillipa, a petite blonde in her late twenties, with dancing blue eyes, offered them a sunny smile.

'Louise, hi!' she exclaimed in welcome, drawing them inside and accepting the present Louise offered. 'Thank you very much, and it's great to see you.'

While Louise was struggling for something to say, Marcus arrived. As dark as his wife was blonde, tall and of medium build, he grinned broadly as he greeted Louise.

'And who's this, Louise?' he teased. 'Where have you been hiding him?'

Over a murmur of voices coming from their lounge, Louise made the introductions.

To her despair, she found the cover story slipped out with deceptive ease, and whatever her inner turmoil, it clearly didn't show, because Phillipa and Marcus accepted it without suspicion and even went so far as to tease her how romantic it was that Dan should come so far to find her. Louise felt acutely uncomfortable, and she did not like being able to lie so easily. It made her feel like such a fraud.

They joined the rest of the guests,

and after offering them some drinks, Marcus departed to put some music on the elaborate CD system. Louise looked around the room with a new frame of mind, wondering if it had been illegal money that had paid for their plush lifestyle.

True to his word, Dan was attentive — almost too attentive, Louise worried, smouldering under the frequent touch of his gaze, her skin permanently sensitised from his hand resting at the small of her back, or his fingers closing around hers, or his arm around her shoulders holding her against him.

It disturbed her resolve.

And he did it all so unconsciously, with such easy familiarity, that she could almost believe that he meant it. Only she knew better.

As the evening wore on, she discovered that though it had been difficult to be friendly and normal with Phillipa and Marcus, her awkwardness abated as Dan had suggested it would. She glanced up at him.

His support and understanding had helped, as did the approval she now found in his eyes as he met her gaze.

'You're doing great,' he praised as he bent his head to whisper in her ear.

Louise turned slightly towards him and he curled an arm round her waist.

'I don't like this,' she whispered back.

'I know.'

He took her hand in his, this thumb tracing featherlight circles in her palm.

'Louise, I want us to — '

'Come on you two, mingle a little,' Marcus's cheerful voice interrupted. 'You haven't taken your hands off each other all evening!'

Louise managed a smile, and for a while they complied with their host's suggestion. They danced, and being held close to him as he guided her round the floor played havoc with her composure, and when the music finished, they joined the other guests and chatted over a buffet supper.

It was just after midnight when Dan

drew her to one side, and unnoticed, he led her from the room and down the hallway.

'Where are we going?'

'The study.'

'But — '

Dan laid his fingers against her mouth, his expression warning her to silence. Unhappily, she accompanied him, the noise of the gathering in the lounge beginning to diminish the farther through the house they went.

Louise managed to stifle a startled protest, her eyes widening, as Dan took something from his pocket and picked the lock of the study door.

He pushed her inside and followed close behind.

'Aren't you meant to have a search warrant for this kind of thing?' she hissed at him, annoyed when he merely offered her a half smile in the dimness. 'Dan . . .'

'What makes you think I haven't got one?'

The enigmatic reply silenced her.

She stared at him, shadowed in the moonlit room, and chewed her lower lip with her teeth.

'Stay here,' Dan instructed, positioning her beside the door which he left ajar. 'If you hear or see anything, come and tell me. Don't make a noise.'

She knew it was futile to challenge him or the way he issued orders to her. Annoyed, she watched as he took a pencil torch from his pocket and crossed to the large, leather-topped desk.

He made a methodical search through the papers, and the drawers, she noticed with a frown, as he picked those locks as well, careful to refasten them afterwards.

Her heart was thudding at the thought of what they were doing, what would happen if they were caught.

She glanced furtively into the corridor, her ears straining for the slightest sound of anyone's approach. When she glanced back at Dan, he was taking something from his pocket and feeling round the desk.

He checked the radiator by the window, then moved to the bookcase that travelled the length of one wall. Louise half edged towards him, then hesitated. What was that?

Her pulse racing, she turned back to the door. Through the crack, she saw Marcus leave the lounge and open the front door to admit a man she couldn't identify.

She was about to sigh with relief, imagining the new arrival was a delayed guest, but the two men walked passed the lounge door and headed towards her. She could hear their voices.

She forced her trembling limbs to carry her from her post and across to Dan. As if he had sensed her approach, he was adjusting something at the bookcase, and by the time she reached him, he had discarded his jacket, his hands taking hold of her and pulling her against him.

'I — '

Her words were choked off as his

mouth closed over hers. He artfully manoeuvred her to a nearby leather sofa and pushed her down, his weight following, holding her in place.

Her efforts to struggle were futile. She felt his hands moving swiftly, first in her hair, then over her clothes.

His kiss intensified, stealing her breath, raising her already racing pulse, and putting paid to any remaining shreds of commonsense she had left.

Louise forgot where she was, why she was there, forgot everything except Dan and the way he made her feel. Every part of her body responded to him; the subtle scent of his aftershave, the passionate persuasiveness of his lips, the feel of his hand against her skin.

Suddenly, the door opened and the light snapped on. The kiss ended abruptly, and her eyes opened.

She blinked against the unaccustomed brightness, her gaze focusing dazedly on Dan's face inches from her own. As if from a great distance, she heard Marcus's voice, amused and conspiratorial.

'Oops! Sorry. Really, Louise, couldn't you wait to get him home?'

Louise didn't have to feign her shocked expression, nor the tide of embarrassed colour that flooded her face at having been caught in such a passionate embrace — no matter how much of a sham it had been. To her it had become too real. Her heart cannoned under her ribs, the breath burned in her lungs, her senses reeled.

Dan moved, rising to his feet and began to smooth down his own clothes. He ran his fingers through his hair in a half-hearted attempt to restore some order to its wildly tousled appearance, then reached out a hand to assist her to her feet.

With more haste than dignity, Louise stood, her knees quaking alarmingly. She dreaded to imagine how rumpled she looked. Discreetly, she smoothed down her wrinkled skirt, then her fingers rose to brush back her wayward hair. Thanks to Dan's rapid stage management, she must look a picture of abandonment.

Dan was clever, she had to give him that.

He had effectively removed any suspicion about why they had sneaked in here together. Or had he? While Marcus still looked amused, the man behind him did not:

The glint of mistrust and malice gleamed in his cold, black eyes. Louise shivered in reaction as she came under their scrutiny, overwhelmed by an impression of danger and latent cruelty.

Was this Ramon? Instinctively she reached for Dan's hand, relieved when his fingers returned a steady pressure.

Dan could feel the tremble in Louise's fingers as she slipped her hand into his.

Damn it, what was Ramon doing in England? How had he got passed all the people who were supposed to be watching out for him? And why hadn't someone warned him of his arrival? His whole body tensed, wary, watchful.

Ramon being here put a whole new perspective on things, and it raised the stakes and the risks. He cursed himself for getting Louise so involved. Just as he was considering how best to handle the situation, Louise spoke, and he was amazed at the calmness and humour in her voice.

'I'm sorry, Marcus, you're right, we should have just slipped home.' She smiled and cast a teasing glance at Dan. 'That's what comes of being involved with a red-blooded Australian! The door was open and — '

'Was it?'

Dan drew Louise against him as Ramon's harsh, accented challenge cut across her explanation. He watched as Ramon turned a sceptical gaze from Louise to Marcus.

'I thought you always kept this room locked, Marcus.'

'Usually,' Marcus agreed lightly,

seeming unperturbed. 'If Louise says it was open, I must have forgotten in the rush of the evening.'

Dan began to guide Louise to the door.

'We'll get out of your way.'

'Aren't you going to introduce us to your friend?' Louise queried, resting a restraining hand on Dan's chest. 'I don't believe we've me, Mr . . . ?'

Marcus cleared his throat.

'Louise, Dan, this is a friend of ours, Miguel.'

Dan took an angry breath as Louise extended her hand to Ramon. What on earth did she think she was doing?

'Louise, we should go,' he insisted, his fingers tightening warningly on hers.

'Where are you from, Miguel?' she queried, ignoring his warning as he hustled her towards the door. 'Are you in antiques like Marcus and Phillipa?'

'We do business, yes,' he replied coldly.

'It must be interesting. How long are you here?'

Ramon's eyes glittered coldly.

'Why?'

'I was going to suggest you come to dinner with Marcus and Phillipa, it — '

'Louise, you can make arrangements another time,' Dan interrupted, taut with anger.

He'd had enough of Louise playing amateur detective.

'Good-night, Marcus, great party. We'll leave you to make our excuses to Phillipa. I think it's about time we went home.'

He ushered Louise out into the corridor and closed his fingers around her arm. Grim-faced, he marched her to the front door, ignoring her struggles as they traversed the Whiteheads' gravel drive and walked the short distance home.

'You're hurting me,' she hissed as he opened the front door and all but shoved her inside.

'What did you think you were playing at?' he demanded furiously, letting her go and pacing up and down the hall. 'Ramon is a nasty piece of work, unpredictable, cruel, dangerous.

'Don't ever forget that. He has no respect for anybody, and stops at nothing to get what he wants.'

'I thought I was helping.'

Dan stopped his pacing and looked at her.

'You were playing with fire. Don't try something like that again. I don't want you in the middle of this.'

'You should have thought of that before you involved me.'

She was right. It was his fault. This investigation was in danger of getting out of hand, and he was in danger of allowing his growing feelings for Louise to play havoc with his professionalism.

Where was his self-discipline? He glared at Louise, angry with her for being so attractive and for tying him up in knots.

Louise returned Dan's angry stare, her jaw firm with mutinous determination. Who did he think he was ordering her around, treating her like an idiot? If she had been a bit reckless this evening, it was his fault for scrambling her brain with that assault on her senses.

She hadn't asked to be caught up in this web of deceit, but now that she was, she refused to be cast into the background. If Dan didn't like it, it was tough luck.

Without another word, she flounced past him and went upstairs, closing her bedroom door with a satisfying bang.

Smarting, she removed the cocktail dress Dan had admired and returned it to the wardrobe, then she removed her make-up and prepared for bed, a frown on her face as she reviewed the events of the evening. Dan had pretty much steam-rollered her into what had happened. And he was far too fond of issuing orders and bossing her around.

As she slid under the duvet, an involuntary shiver went through her as she remembered Miguel Ramon's hard, cold face, and his cruel eyes. She could well believe Dan's insistence the South American was a dangerous man.

She hoped she never saw him again. The sooner this was over, the happier she would be.

★ ★ ★

She dozed fitfully until a faint noise woke her. The room was still dark, and she glanced at her bedside clock, the luminous dial showing her it was a few minutes short of four in the morning.

She listened intently.

Yes, she could definitely hear Dan's footsteps on the landing. At least, she hoped it was Dan.

Louise slipped from the bed and crept along to the top of the stairs. She saw a brief glimmer of light from the kitchen before it flicked out quickly. She tiptoed softly down the stairs.

'Dan?' she whispered, seeing his shadow in the dimness. 'What's happened?'

'Why are you whispering?'

His husky voice contained an edge of humour. Suddenly, the light snapped on, and Louise blinked against the glare.

'I thought . . . '

She stopped her mumbled explanation as her gaze focused betrayingly on his body. She swallowed and dragged her gaze away.

He smiled, sensing her awareness and discomfort.

'I came down for a glass of milk.'

'Oh.'

Her gaze met the sultriness of his. She felt like an idiot and cursed the vividness of her imagination.

Self-consciously, she raised a hand to the neckline of her flimsy cotton nightgown, suddenly aware how under-dressed she was.

His watchful gaze followed the nervous movement of her fingers. Louise clenched them in a fist at her throat and took an involuntary step back as Dan set down his drained glass and moved towards her.

'I'll go back up then,' she murmured. 'I'm sorry if I woke you.'

'It's too hot to sleep,' she said as she continued to edge away from him.

He continued to peruse her.

She felt the wall behind her and glanced anxiously for a means of escape. Dan stepped up close, too close, and flattened one hand on the wall beside her head.

She could feel the heat from his body, smell his earthy fragrance.

The predatory way he had stalked her and now looked at her was alarming. Louise sucked much-needed air into her lungs. There was this smouldering sensuality about him he made no effort to check.

'Perhaps you need to take a cool shower.'

Louise was convinced her heart actually stopped for several beats following his throaty suggestion before it resumed at a frantic pace.

Her gazed flicked to his chest and

saw a faint sheen of perspiration on his skin.

'I don't really think so,' she finally managed to reply, her tone as convincing as she could make it.

He ran the back of one hand agonisingly along the line of her jaw.

'I could make you change your mind.'

'I bet you couldn't.'

'How much?'

Her throat tightened.

'It was a figure of speech.'

'You issue challenges like that and I'll be tempted to take them up,' he warned her silkily.

His hand moved along her neck to shape itself to the back of her head, tangling in her chestnut hair.

When he leaned closer and brushed a kiss to the corner of her mouth, she fought against the effect he had on her.

She was determined to maintain her self control. His lips moved to the other corner, teasing, threatening her resolve.

She raised her hands to push him away, but her traitorous fingers lingered, enjoying the feel of his skin and the dusting of hair.

At her touch, he murmured her name, his lips closing more insistently on hers.

Disobeying her instructions, her hands crept up to his shoulders, bringing him closer to her instead of pushing him away, his kiss blotting out reason.

When he raised his hands to her wrists and removed her hold on him, he pulled back, his voice a husky taunt against her ear.

'You just lost your money. Sleep well,' he added, stepping away from her and walking from the room.

Louise remained in the kitchen, her body trembling.

Tears of frustration and anger stung her eyes. How could she let him do this to her when she knew it was nothing but a game to him?

He was playing with her feelings, but she meant nothing to him other than an amusing diversion. Her body's responses to each look, each touch, were allowing him to get away with it. Where was her pride?

9

Did you get some sleep?' Dan asked when he walked into the kitchen the next morning.

'Yes, thank you,' she lied in response to his query, turning her back as he walked across to the fridge and took out a carton of milk. 'You?'

She felt his gaze on her as she washed her empty coffee cup and set it on the drainer.

'Not much. I kept dreaming of you.'

His heated words aroused an immediate response within her, as if he was actually touching her.

She determined to ignore it, refusing to allow him to manipulate her. Turning to face him, she saw the mix of amusement and desire in his eyes, took a deep breath, and pressed ahead with her carefully rehearsed speech. She'd spent most of the night thinking it up.

'Dan, I can't change the fact that you are here to do a job. And I can't change the fact you think you have an effect on me, but I have no intention of entering into any kind of relationship with you.'

She paused for a moment, her gaze unwilling to lock with his.

'I will do what is necessary to assist you with the investigation, but that's all. There is to be no repeat of last night. Soon you will be gone from my life. Until then, your dreams will have to satisfy you.'

Amazed at the quiet control of her voice, she was further surprised to see Dan swallow, and to witness what appeared suspiciously like disappointment in his eyes before he masked it.

'If that's what you want.'

His quiet response to her statement gave her no sense of victory. Instead, the flatness of his voice had her biting her lip, a frown of confusion furrowing her brow.

He sounded resigned, almost defeated, as he turned away from her and took a bowl and packet of cereal from a cupboard.

'Well, I'll leave you to your breakfast then,' she continued after a momentary hesitation. 'I'm going out for a walk.'

★ ★ ★

Louise crossed the garden and unlocked the gate that gave access to the private woodland that ran along the back of the estate.

It was cool and shady under the trees, a welcome relief from the heat and glare of the sun of the last couple of weeks. But she had no respite from her thoughts.

All she seemed to be able to think about lately was Dan. For all her fancy words in the kitchen just now, what frightened her was if she really wanted to hold him at bay.

He had said he did whatever it took to get his job done. Did that include her? Was she just a tool for him to get what he wanted? Had he ever meant any of the things he had said to her?

She acknowledged with discomfort that she had reached the stage where she wanted him to mean it, where he was becoming important to her. Too important. It made her vulnerable.

She had no intention of ever depending on anyone for her happiness and well-being. And despite her anger and distrust at the way he had lied his way into her home and her life, she feared he had found his way into her heart as well.

As she walked on, scarcely aware of the birdlife and flowers around her, the distant sounds of voices drew her from her reverie. She walked on, and the voices grew louder.

Through the trees, she recognised Marcus and Ramon, their figures hunched over the ground.

Her heart began to thud.

As quietly as possible, terrified her presence would be discovered, she crept into the undergrowth of bracken and shrubby growth.

From her position, she could not see exactly what the men were doing, but it looked as if Ramon was checking something — a package wrapped in black plastic.

He stood up, but Marcus remained crouched on the ground. Louise saw Ramon pass the package back and Marcus placed it in the hole in front of him and carefully moved earth and a covering of leaves and debris back over it, adding a decaying log as a finishing touch.

She could not make out what they were saying, but as they walked back in the direction of the Whiteheads' house, they passed nearer her, and she shrank back, trying to pick up a few words.

'. . . set to come back here tonight,' Marcus finished.

'Yes, we must move. I don't like coincidences. Finish it.'

The harsh brutality of Ramon's voice made her cringe. When their voices had faded, and she could no longer see or hear them, Louise eased her cramped limbs and stood up.

After making sure she had her bearings and would recognise the spot again, she hurried back to the house to tell Dan.

* * *

Dan sat close to the open window in his room and wrote up his notes on what had happened the previous night.

That included any scrap of information he had been able to glean from his search of Marcus's study.

They had been interrupted before he could complete all he wanted to do but at least he had placed a listening device that would transmit information to a surveillance van parked on the public road within range of the transmitter.

He had spoken with the Chief and expressed his displeasure at coming face to face with Ramon.

Norman Curry was now in a rage that the Colombian had been able to slip into the country undetected but as long as things were tightened up pretty quickly, Dan wasn't bothered whose heads were rolling.

He had taken several photographs with the camera he had set up, the powerful lens giving him good shots of Ramon with the Whiteheads. For all the problems, at least it was solid evidence of their involvement. When Ramon left the estate, the tails would be waiting to track him and this time, Dan hoped the net would close in to bring an end to this case — and that nothing would go wrong.

He forced himself to concentrate on what he was doing, and not to allow his mind to dwell on Louise and her speech in the kitchen. While he respected her for sticking up for herself, he didn't believe she was as emotionally immune to him as she wanted to think.

Although he continued to chastise

himself for not backing off and the warning bells continued to sound, he could not stop wanting her.

'Dan?'

He rose as he heard Louise's anxious call, and opened his door in time to see her running up the stairs, breathless, her face flushed. Concern gripped him.

'Are you OK?'

'Yes,' she gasped, placing a hand on her chest. 'I'm fine. Listen, I've just seen Ramon and Marcus in the woods.'

Instantly he was tense.

He drew her into his room and took his seat by the window to keep a watch on the house.

'Tell me exactly what happened,' he instructed, listening intently as she explained in detail what she had seen and heard.

'I know it isn't much,' she finished with a nervous smile. 'I hope it helps.'

'It does, thanks. Are you sure they didn't see you?'

'Positive. I was really careful.'

Dan nodded and tapped a sheet of paper absently against his chin, a frown of consideration puckering his brow.

Louise had taken a risk, and it gave him a real fright to think what could have happened had she been seen.

He didn't want to frighten her, but Ramon was crazy and very dangerous, and for all his outward charm and friendliness, he didn't doubt for a second that Marcus Whitehead would protect his own interests if it became necessary.

'Do you want me to show you the exact spot?' she asked.

'No.'

'What are you going to do?'

'I'll call it in,' he told her in businesslike tones, turning back to the window so she wouldn't be able to read his feelings.

'All right.'

She rose to her feet and moved towards the door. She had sounded disappointed, a little hurt at his brusque manner, and he hated that he had been the cause.

'Louise . . . '

'Yes?'

She lingered, but he held back the words he had been going to say.

'There was a telephone call from Australia, but I figured you wouldn't want me to answer it. The message is on the machine,' he told her lamely, inwardly cursing himself for being such a fool.

'Thank you.'

Dan sighed as she shut the door behind her, and once he had heard her descending the stairs, he reached for his mobile phone.

He needed to talk to Norman Curry and plan what looked to be a night of watching in the woods. If what Louise had heard was correct, he would need to be there, hidden with the right equipment, ready for when Ramon and Marcus returned to their cache.

That evening, as dusk fell, Louise sat in her study and tried to compose a letter to her family in Australia.

The message on the answer machine had assured her that her mother had made a complete recovery and they had continued the holiday before returning to Sydney. What worried her was the second part of the message which conveyed Greg's concern about 'her little problem' and the news he had decided to do some checking.

Fearing he would ring back if she didn't respond soon to say all was well, she had decided to send a note of reassurance rather than face an inquisition by phone and be placed in the position of lying about Dan.

Louise toyed with her pen, unable to concentrate on her task. She hadn't seen Dan since she had left his room.

He had been out for an hour or so during the afternoon, and although she had heard him return to his room, they had not established any contact. Tension permeated the atmosphere and she was on edge, wondering what the next step in this operation would be.

With a sigh, she glanced out of her window at the gathering darkness and rose to draw her curtains.

She tensed when she saw a dark figure creep through the shadows of the garden towards the gate that led to the woods. Anxiety knotted her stomach. She could not shake off the knowledge that Dan could be putting himself in danger.

As the minutes dragged to half an hour, and half an hour to an hour, Louise's anxiety increased.

She abandoned her letter and paced about the house, unable to settle. For a while, she tried to read, then watched some television but it failed to hold her interest.

* * *

As one hour became two and still the clock ticked on, she began pacing again, until by the time midnight had come and gone, she could no longer stand the wait.

What if something had happened and Dan was lying hurt in the woods? If he needed help and she had done nothing, she would never forgive herself.

All right, she allowed as she went up to her room, he was a highly-trained professional, but that didn't guarantee his safety one hundred per cent. He had said himself that Ramon was dangerous and would stop at nothing to get what he wanted.

She changed rapidly into dark clothes and pulled on a pair of old trainers before turning out the lights and going downstairs.

She left the house, waiting a few moments to allow her eyes to adjust to the night. There was no moon to guide her path, but familiarity and instinct led her to the woods.

Once under the canopy, the blackness closed in around her and she felt the first thread of alarm.

Rustlings in the undergrowth made her jump, and the penetrating call of an owl saw her covering her mouth to silence the startled exclamation that threatened to betray her presence.

She edged carefully along the rough trail, pausing frequently to check for noises or signs of Dan.

How far she had strayed into the wood she could not tell but she was beginning to worry if she could ever find him. Maybe this hadn't been such a good idea.

Gingerly she moved forward, her hand reaching out to press against the trunk of a tree and balance her as she stumbled over an exposed root. She held back a curse.

She was about to straighten when, without warning, she was grabbed from behind and a gloved hand clamped roughly over her mouth.

10

Shock drove the breath from Louise's lungs and terrified her. As panic set in, she began to struggle, but her assailant pushed her sharply back against the tree, sandwiching her between the rough bark and a solid, male body. How had he known where to find her in the darkness?

'Are you insane?' Dan hissed angrily. 'What are you doing here?'

The pressure of the hand covering her mouth relaxed and she was able to respond.

'When you didn't come back, I thought — '

Louise smarted with the anger of injustice. How dare he? His cold, hard-edged manner scared her and she struggled to push herself away from him but he refused to release her.

'Do you think I haven't enough on

161

my mind out here without you to worry about as well?'

Before she could respond to his stinging rebuke, the pressure of his body against hers increased and as she made a protest, his hand clamped over her mouth once more.

'Stand still. Be quiet.'

Hearing a distant sound, Louise froze.

In the blackness, she could just distinguish the flickering beams of light that had alerted Dan.

Dan looked at the twin spots of light with a moment of grim satisfaction. If that was Ramon and Marcus, one concern that they may have similar night vision equipment to his own was removed. His revised priority now was to get Louise hidden out of harm's way.

This was all he needed to mess up his plans.

'Do exactly what I tell you, when I tell you,' he mouthed harshly against her ear. 'Understand?'

He felt her nod, and grasping her arm firmly, he fixed his night sight back in place and drew her away from the path.

Trying to move as silently as he wanted was impossible and he tried to be patient, knowing Louise could not see. But whose fault was that he thought sourly.

At first, he hadn't believed it when Louise had come stumbling along the path, feeling her way in the dark.

By rights, he should now be safe in the lair he had prepared, infrared film waiting to roll and record evidence against Ramon and Marcus, not dragging some hare-brained female deeper into the woods. Torn between worrying about Louise and his need to be at his station in time, he hastily picked out a suitable hiding place.

'Get down,' he instructed, shoving her into the cover of a deep thicket without preamble.

He squatted down, able to see her frightened face, and cursed under his breath. He didn't have time for this.

'Whatever happens, you are not to move an inch until I come back for you,' he insisted.

Then he melted away into the darkness.

★ ★ ★

The torch beams were drawing closer and he only made it back to his position with a couple of minutes to spare. He slid into cover, did an instinctive re-check of his equipment and lay motionless, waiting, watching as Ramon and Marcus approached.

He started the film as they began to uncover their cache, capturing the moment they took several plastic-wrapped packages from the ground.

This time, he acknowledged with a satisfied smile, Ramon and his sidekicks were not going to get away.

A few more minutes, and he could follow them back to the house. The recordings of their conversations in

Marcus's study, combined with his film and the rest of the evidence they had painstakingly collated over the months and months pursuing Ramon would finally bring an end to their sordid criminal activities.

* * *

Louise waited where Dan had left her, sure the thudding of her heart could be heard for miles around.

He had vanished as stealthily as he had appeared, and she felt alone and scared in the uncomfortable hideaway he had found for her. The blackness as smothering.

She had no idea what was happening, where Dan was, but every sound was magnified and spooked her strained nerves.

Unable to judge the passing of time, she began to try and count off the minutes, but sixty seconds felt like a lifetime, and she soon gave up the task.

When a gunshot exploded in the

stillness of the night, Louise jumped and smothered a scream.

A second retort, closer this time, shattered the air, and sent unseen creatures scuttling for cover.

Dan?

Unheedful of his parting instructions, Louise rose to her feet. She could not see anything, but numb with fear for him, she scrambled and stumbled in the direction he had taken when he had left her.

Brambles scratched her skin and tore at her clothes but she kept going, driven by her desperation to find Dan and make sure he was safe.

Tears stung her eyes and a sob escaped at the thought of him being hurt. She hastened blindly on, a sharp scream escaping as a torch snapped on trapping her in its glare.

To her horror, Ramon's face was illuminated before her.

'You make a nuisance of yourself,' Ramon snapped icily, catching hold of her.

166

'Let me go,' Louise demanded, fear and anxiety bringing a rise to her voice.

She stumbled as Ramon thrust her forward.

'Where are you taking me?'

Ramon ignored her and turned to Marcus.

'Bring the bag to the house.'

The painful grip of Ramon's fingers bit into her flesh, but Louise steeled herself to betray no more outward displays of protest or fear. She glanced over her shoulder and saw Marcus's torch beam bobbing along the path behind. Where was Dan?

A tear escaped to trickle down her cheek. If anything had happened to him . . . She tried to blank out the thought.

★ ★ ★

Dan struggled to sit up, clenching his teeth at the searing pain in his right leg. He swore viciously under his breath, anger boiling inside him — especially at Louise.

Couldn't the crazy woman ever do what she was told?

No-one had been shooting at him.

Did she think he was stupid enough to stand up and give Ramon free target practice? Damn it.

The shots had come from his left — poachers, most likely.

The next thing he knew, Louise was crashing through the undergrowth. He had taken off to halt her headlong flight towards danger without grabbing his night sight. He hadn't seen the ditch.

Gritting his teeth against the fiery agony in his leg, he began the long, painful crawl to the house. He had to get help before something terrible happened to Louise. A fresh pain gripped him in the vicinity of his heart. If Louise was hurt . . . Filled with renewed determination, he hastened his progress.

★ ★ ★

Louise sat on the leather sofa in Marcus's study, her body shaking with fright. Marcus, so different from the easy-going man she had once thought she knew, was packing things from his desk into a briefcase. He glanced at her angrily, a sneer in his voice.

'You should have minded your own business, Louise.'

She looked at him with troubled eyes, but did not reply. Not only had she failed to find Dan, she was now in danger herself.

If she had ever had the slightest doubts about the investigation and Dan's repeated warnings these people were dangerous, they had evaporated in the last hours.

Her eyes closed briefly and she bit her lip, praying Dan was not lying hurt somewhere — or worse. A sob welled in her throat but she choked it down.

As the study door opened, she turned her head and ice cold threads of fear prickled her spine as Ramon entered the room and walked purposefully towards her.

She shrank back from him, but he captured her chin in a vice-like grip.

'Why were you in the woods? Who or what were you looking for?'

Tears stung her eyes at the pressure of Ramon's fingers, but she stubbornly refused to answer his questions. No matter what they did to her, she would not betray the man she loved. The inner knowledge was a shock. But just as she now acknowledged the depth of her feelings, she feared it may already be too late.

'Who does your boyfriend work for?'

'An imports and exports company in Australia,' she said, instinctively sticking to the cover story in a desperate attempt to protect Dan should he be alive and undetected.

Ramon tightened his hold, hurting her, his cruel eyes looking into hers.

'I would enjoy making you tell me all you know.'

'I don't know anything. What do you

mean? What is all this about?'

'You lie.'

Ramon shoved her roughly aside, then turned to Marcus.

'There is no time to waste. The boat awaits us.'

'What about her? Do we take her with us?'

The sound of Phillipa's harsh enquiry from the doorway made Louise gasp. She met her former friend's gaze, but the blue eyes held no hint of friendship or compassion. Louise stifled a whimper as Ramon pulled a gun from his waistband, an evil smile on his face as he ran the cold barrel down her cheek. She had never seen a gun before, except on the television, and they did not improve with closer acquaintance.

She felt suddenly cold and very frightened.

'No,' Ramon answered Phillipa's question. 'We leave her here. By the time she is found we will be gone. It is but a minor inconvenience to bring our plans forward.'

'And the boyfriend?' Marcus asked, snapping the briefcase closed and walking across the room.

'He can do nothing to us now.'

Ramon's words appeared to confirm her fears and she gave a shocked cry.

'Go to the car,' Ramon ordered, and without a backward glance, Marcus and Phillipa departed.

Left along with Ramon, Louise stared up at him through tear-filled eyes, and a strange calmness enveloped her.

She watched as Ramon raised the gun. There was a moment of hesitation, then a shot reverberated around the room.

11

Are you meant to be on that leg?
You're not going to be much use to
anyone if you damage it permanently.'

Dan scowled in response to Norman
Curry's remarks and lowered himself
on to a chair, thrusting his unwieldy
crutches aside with a growl of irritation.
Three days they had kept him in that
damn hospital while they had pinned
and plastered his leg.

Three days when all he had wanted
to do was go to Louise, at least to hear
her voice.

And now he was out, supposedly to
rest, but how could he rest when there
was only the answer machine to talk to
at Louise's, when she never returned
his calls?

Where was she?

Or was she there, and she just didn't
want to talk to him? A knife twisted

inside him at the thought.

He met the Chief's ice-blue stare, his own eyes filled with impatience.

'Well?' he prompted, his irritation at the world in general increasing.

'A few discreet enquiries furnished me with the information you wanted,' the Chief said brusquely.

'Thanks,' Dan muttered, glancing at the paper the older man handed to him before he folded it and shoved it in his jeans' pocket.

'Are you sure about this? You're not fit.'

'I'm fine.'

Norman Curry shook his head in resignation.

'Keep in touch.'

'Sure thing.'

Heaving the crutches into use once more, Dan stood up, pausing at the door to glance back.

'Thanks, Chief.'

Norman Curry watched Dan hobble from the office, allowing himself a momentary smile of satisfaction. The case was closed and watertight — his unit had done a first-rate job, which was exactly what he expected of them.

Just now, he had witnessed something he had least expected. He had seen the first genuine emotion disturb the usually poker-faced control of the man who sat opposite him.

The woman had got to him. Who would have believed it? Maverick Dan was human after all.

★ ★ ★

It was a lazy Sunday, with temperatures in the mid-seventies. Eyes closed, Louise lay back on her lounger beside the pool at the rear of Greg's and Ginny's Sydney suburbs home, and listened to the children's laughter as they dashed around the garden.

She had been here for a week. Every day had been a struggle. Every moment, she had battled to present a normal front to her family and pretend that nothing was wrong, endeavoured to smile and laugh, and give no hint of the real reason why she had abandoned her own summer and spring this surprise visit on them.

As yet, she had not found a way to break the news to her parents about Phillipa and Marcus who were both in custody and facing several charges. With the substantial evidence against them, they faced a lengthy stay in prison. Louise could not say she was sorry.

The night of the ordeal in Marcus's study, was fresh in her mind. She could still hear the sound of the shot, still recall those first moments when she realised there was no pain, that it was Ramon's body that crumpled to the floor — that it was another gun that had fired. The marksman's skilful shot had disarmed, not killed.

What followed had passed in a blur. The house had been swarming with police and members of Norman Curry's unit.

Phillipa and Marcus had been taken

away to be questioned, while Ramon had travelled under guard to have his wound attended at hospital before he, too, would be incarcerated.

Norman Curry himself had taken her home, made her tea, been perfectly solicitous. He had explained that Marcus's study had been bugged, that a team was already on standby for Dan's surveillance in the woods that night and they had moved in the instant they had realised what was happening.

He had taken her statement, told her Dan had not been shot and then he had gone.

To him, it was over. Only for her, it wasn't. There was still Dan.

'What's wrong?'

Greg's soft-voiced query brought her eyes open, and she shaded them against the sun to stare up at him.

'Nothing,' she lied, swallowing at the concern and disbelief on his face.

'Louise,' he chided, sitting on a chair beside her. 'Can't you tell me?

You've been withdrawn and unhappy since you arrived. Oh, I know,' he added, correctly reading her alarmed expression. 'You've tried to hide it, but we can all see you're not yourself.'

Louise debated telling him that the Whiteheads had been arrested, but decided against it.

That would entail telling him details, and she couldn't face it, not yet. She flicked her gaze to his and away again.

'I'm fine.'

'Is it anything to do with that man you mentioned, the one who came to the house?'

A frown creased Greg's brow at her start of shock.

'Did he hurt you?'

'Of course not.'

Louise tried to laugh but the attempt failed. She rolled on to her front to evade Greg's probing gaze.

'I'm just tired after the flight and the hectic school year, that's all. The break with you will work wonders.'

She knew Greg was not satisfied, but was thankful when he settled back and did not pursue the subject.

She blinked away a sudden welling of tears. Yes, Dan had hurt her. He had turned her life upside down, broken her heart in the process, then he had left without a word of goodbye.

12

It had been a major wrench to find that one of Norman Curry's men had removed all of Dan's personal things from the house. There had been no news, no contact.

Gradually, the realisation had sunk in. Dan was not coming back.

She had waited three days, hoping she might hear something from him. Three days during which the house had felt empty and strange. Three days when her emotions had travelled from bitter disappointment, anger, hurt, loneliness and all stations in between.

More than once she had tried to tell herself that a relationship founded on deception and mistrust could have no chance of survival. It didn't stop her loving him. There had been no promise of anything at all.

When the job was done, he walked

away. She knew that. It didn't stop her loving him. She told herself she was successful, independent, that she didn't need Dan. It didn't stop her loving him.

Who was the real Dan? His surface, his tough persona had cracked several times to reveal a vulnerable, warm, caring inner core. But had he ever meant a single thing he had said to her, or was it all an act, part of the cover to win her over?

The whole experience had altered her. She doubted she would ever be able to view their quiet, backwater estate in the same light again. She knew for a fact that she would be wary of trusting her friendships so easily in the future and that saddened her. But most of all, Dan had changed her. She felt only half alive without him.

Once, she had gone to the Guildford office where he had taken her the day she had discovered he was not who he said he was. But the office was bare, no trace of the unit existed.

She realised she had no idea where they were based, even what their full title was. Nor did she know where Dan lived. After three days, she had made herself face facts. Dan was not going to call. He was gone. She would never see him again.

When the note had arrived from Norman Curry, enclosing a cheque in recompense for her expenses, it had been the final straw. It had made her feel cheap, as if she had sold herself in some way.

There had been no return address, so Louise had vented her fury by ripping the cheque to shreds.

No money, no platitudes, could compensate for the loss of Dan. No amount could be high enough to help her mend her broken heart.

'Louise!'

Her sister's voice roused her from her contemplation, and she rolled on to her back with a sigh.

'Yes?' she asked, trying to shake the

listless feeling that transferred itself to her voice.

'Aren't you even going to say hello?'

The mocking drawl had her jerking into a sitting position. Her eyes opened wide with shock and disbelief as she stared at Dan as if he was an apparition. Stunned, she took in his tousled appearance, his stubble jaw, his jean-clad figure — the plaster cast that encased his right leg from foot to knee, and the crutches that supported him as she stood on the lawn a few yards away.

Her heart constricted.

'You're hurt.'

'Thanks to you.'

'Me?' she exclaimed. 'What did I do?'

'The opposite of what I told you . . . as usual.'

A tinge of colour suffused her cheeks. 'When the gun went off, I — '

'Gun?' Greg demanded beside her. 'What gun? What's going on?'

Louise barely heard him. All her

attention was focused on the man she loved, the man she had thought she would never see again.

'I tried to intercept you and fell down a ditch,' Dan explained patiently, then shifted his weight with a grimace. 'And now I'm here, and I hate planes, and my leg aches, and I haven't even had a proper welcome from the woman I love.'

Uncaring that her bewildered family looked on, Louise dashed across the space that separated them into his embrace.

Dan balanced himself on one crutch and wrapped his free arm around her, holding her tight against him. She was so lovely, her bikini-clad body so graceful, the familiar scent of lilacs stirring him as he buried his face in her hair. He never intended to let her go again.

Coming back to Australia, particularly to Sydney, had been hard — there were so many bad memories. But Louise was here, and that was all that mattered.

He felt her tears against his skin, and pulled back to kiss the wetness from her face.

'Don't cry, Louise. Everything's all right now.'

'Dan, I thought you'd gone. You didn't call, I had no idea where you were. I never expected to see you again.'

He smiled and gave her a lingering kiss.

'I was in hospital. As soon as I could, I rang and rang. I thought you were glad it was over, that you were avoiding me. Then I found out you'd flown here.'

'And you came.'

She smiled up at him.

'Don't you know I'd go to the ends of the earth for you?'

'Oh, Dan,' she whispered. 'I didn't know you were hurt. I couldn't get in touch with anyone and I couldn't stay in the house without you. It felt so empty, and I was so lonely.'

'Not any more,' he promised with

heartfelt simplicity.

'Would one of you please tell us what is going on?' Ginny's impatient voice interrupted them.

Dan locked Louise to his side and sent her family his most charming and devilish grin.

'How do you folks feel about planning a wedding?'

He glanced down at Louise's radiant face, her tear-bright brown eyes and kissed her.

He wanted to spend the rest of his life with her, loved her more than he had thought it possible to love another human being — she gave his life meaning, made him whole.

She had been reckless but so brave, and he would never forget the way she had thrown herself into battle for him, faced the danger because she had thought he was hurt, or the way she had tried to protect him.

Fear had been in her voice on the tape he had heard from that night in Marcus's study. But she had been more afraid for him, had lied to protect him and not herself. He had found a treasure and he would never cease to give thanks for the gift.

A sudden thought occurred to him. What were the words in the marriage ceremony? Love, honour and obey?

He smiled against the softness of her mouth. A lot of good the last would do him. The throbbing in his leg reminded him all too clearly that his special lady had a will of her own.

THE END

SAVAGE PARADISE
Sheila Belshaw

For four years, Diana Hamilton had dreamed of returning to Luangwa Valley in Zambia. Now she was back — and, after a close encounter with a rhino — was receiving a lecture from a tall, khaki-clad man on the dangers of going into the bush alone!

PAST BETRAYALS
Giulia Gray

As soon as Jon realized that Julia had fallen in love with him, he broke off their relationship and returned to work in the Middle East. When Jon's best friend, Danny, proposed a marriage of friendship, Julia accepted. Then Jon returned and Julia discovered her love for him remained unchanged.

PRETTY MAIDS ALL IN A ROW
Rose Meadows

The six beautiful daughters of George III of England dreamt of handsome princes coming to claim them, but the King always found some excuse to reject proposals of marriage. This is the story of what befell the Princesses as they began to seek lovers at their father's court, leaving behind rumours of secret marriages and illegitimate children.

THE GOLDEN GIRL
Paula Lindsay

Sarah had everything — wealth, social background, great beauty and magnetic charm. Her heart was ruled by love and compassion for the less fortunate in life. Yet, when one man's happiness was at stake, she failed him — and herself.

A DREAM OF HER OWN
Barbara Best

A stranger gently kisses Sarah Danbury at her Betrothal Ball. Little does she realise that she is to meet this mysterious man again in very different circumstances.

HOSTAGE OF LOVE
Nara Lake

From the moment pretty Emma Tregear, the only child of a Van Diemen's Land magnate, met Philip Despard, she was desperately in love. Unfortunately, handsome Philip was a convict on parole.

THE ROAD TO BENDOUR
Joyce Eaglestone

Mary Mackenzie had lived a sheltered life on the family farm in Scotland. When she took a job in the city she was soon in a romantic maze from which only she could find the way out.

NEW BEGINNINGS
Ann Jennings

On the plane to his new job in a hospital in Turkey, Felix asked Harriet to put their engagement on hold, as Philippe Krir, the Director of Bodrum hospital, refused to hire 'attached' people. But, without an engagement ring, what possible excuse did Harriet have for holding Philippe at bay?

THE CAPTAIN'S LADY
Rachelle Edwards

1820: When Lianne Vernon becomes governess at Elswick Manor, she finds her young pupil is given to strange imaginings and that her employer, Captain Gideon Lang, is the most enigmatic man she has ever encountered. Soon Lianne begins to fear for her pupil's safety.

THE VAUGHAN PRIDE
Margaret Miles

As the new owner of Southwood Manor, Laura Vaughan discovers that she's even more poverty stricken than before. She also finds that her neighbour, the handsome Marius Kerr, is a little too close for comfort.

HONEY-POT
Mira Stables

Lovely, well-born, well-dowered, Russet Ingram drew all men to her. Yet here she was, a prisoner of the one man immune to her graces — accused of frivolously tampering with his young ward's romance!

DREAM OF LOVE
Helen McCabe

When there is a break-in at the art gallery she runs, Jade can't believe that Corin Bossinney is a trickster, or that she'd fallen for the oldest trick in the book . . .

FOR LOVE OF OLIVER
Diney Delancey

When Oliver Scott buys her family home, Carly retains the stable block from which she runs her riding school. But she soon discovers Oliver is not an easy neighbour to have. Then Carly is presented with a new challenge, one she must face for love of Oliver.

THE SECRET OF MONKS' HOUSE
Rachelle Edwards

Soon after her arrival at Monks' House, Lilith had been told that it was haunted by a monk, and she had laughed. Of greater interest was their neighbour, the mysterious Fabian Delamaye. Was he truly as debauched as rumour told, and what was the truth about his wife's death?

THE SPANISH HOUSE
Nancy John

Lynn couldn't help falling in love with the arrogant Brett Sackville. But Brett refused to believe that she felt nothing for his half-brother, Rafael. Lynn knew that the cruel game Brett made her play to protect Rafael's heart could end only by breaking hers.

PROUD SURGEON
Lynne Collins

Calder Savage, the new Senior Surgical Officer at St. Antony's Hospital, had really lived up to his name, venting a savage irony on anyone who fell foul of him. But when he gave Staff Nurse Honor Portland a lift home, she was surprised to find what an interesting man he was.

A PARTNER FOR PENNY
Pamela Forest

Penny had grown up with Christopher Lloyd and saw in him the older brother she'd never had. She was dismayed when he was arrogantly confident that she should not trust her new business colleague, Gerald Hart. She opposed Chris by setting out to win Gerald as a partner both in love and business.

SURGEON ASHORE
Ann Jennings

Luke Roderick, the new Consultant Surgeon for Accident and Emergency, couldn't understand why Staff Nurse Naomi Selbourne refused to apply for the vacant post of Sister. Naomi wasn't about to tell him that she moonlighted as a waitress in order to support her small nephew, Toby.

A MOONLIGHT MEETING
Peggy Gaddis

Megan seemed to have fallen under handsome Tom Fallon's spell, and she was no longer sure if she would be happy as Larry's wife. It was only in the aftermath of a terrible tragedy that she realized the true meaning of love.

THE STARLIT GARDEN
Patricia Hemstock

When interior designer Tansy Donaghue accepted a commission to restore Beechwood Manor in Devon, she was relieved to leave London and its memories of her broken romance with architect Robert Jarvis. But her dream of a peaceful break was shattered not only by Robert's unexpected visit, but also by the manipulative charms of the manor's owner, James Buchanan.

THE BECKONING DAWN
Georgina Ferrand

For twenty-five years Caroline has lived the life of a recluse, believing she is ugly because of a facial scar. After a successful operation, the handsome Anton Tessler comes into her life. However, Caroline soon learns that the kind of love she yearns for may never be hers.

THE WAY OF THE HEART
Rebecca Marsh

It was the scandal of the season when world-famous actress Andrea Lawrence stalked out of a Broadway hit to go home again. But she hadn't jeopardized her career for nothing. The beautiful star was onstage for the play of her life — a drama of double-dealing romance starring her sister's fiancé.

VIENNA MASQUERADE
Lorna McKenzie

In Austria, Kristal Hastings meets Rodolfo von Steinberg, the young cousin of Baron Gustav von Steinberg, who had been her grandmother's lover many years ago. An instant attraction flares between them — but how can Kristal give her love to Rudi when he is already promised to another . . . ?

HIDDEN LOVE
Margaret McDonagh

Until his marriage, Matt had seemed like an older brother to Teresa. Now, five years later, Matt's wife has tragically died and Teresa feels she must go and comfort him. But how much longer can she hold on to the secret that has been hers for all these years?

A MOST UNUSUAL MARRIAGE
Barbara Best

Practically penniless, Dorcas Wareham meets Suzette, who tells her that she had rashly married a Captain Jack Bickley on the eve of his leaving for the Boer War. She suggests that Dorcas takes her place, saying that Jack didn't expect to survive the war anyway. With some misgivings, Dorcas finally agrees. But Jack does return . . .

A TOUCH OF TENDERNESS
Juliet Gray

Ben knew just how to charm, how to captivate a woman — though he could not win a heart that was already in another man's keeping. But Clare was desperately anxious to protect him from a pain she knew too well herself.

NEED FOR A NURSE
Lynne Collins

When Kelvin, a celebrated actor, regained consciousness after a car accident, he had lost his memory. He was shocked to learn that he was engaged to the beautiful actress Beth Hastings. His mind was troubled — and so was his heart when he became aware of the impact on his emotions of a pretty staff nurse . . .

WHISPER OF DOUBT
Rachel Croft

Fiona goes to Culvie Castle to value paintings for the owner, who is in America. After meeting Ewen McDermott, the heir to the castle, Fiona suspects that there is something suspicious going on. But little does she realise what heartache lies ahead of her . . .